The Everlasting
GIFT

David-Matthew Barnes

TRYST
A CAYELLE IMPRINT

The Everlasting GIFT

For permission requests, contact the publisher below:

A CAYÉLLE IMPRINT

Cayélle Publishing/Tryst Imprint
Lancaster, California USA

www.CayellePublishing.com

Orders by U.S. trade bookstores and wholesalers, please contact Freadom Distribution at:
Freadom@Cayelle.com

Categories: 1. Romance 2. Holiday 3. Holiday Romance
Printed in the United States of America

Cover Art by Robin Ludwig Design, Inc.
Interior Design & Typesetting by Ampersand Bookery
Edited by Dr. Mekhala Spencer

ISBN: 978-1-952404-71-9 [paperback]
ISBN: 978-1-952404-67-2 [ebook]

Library of Congress Control Number 2021943572

The Everlasting
GIFT

Acknowledgments

I OFFER MY DEEPEST gratitude to the wonderful people who support my creative efforts, including Aaliyah Moreno, Alfonso Sanchez, Amber Smith Dawson, Amber Ybarra, Amelia Paz, Andrea Patten, Andrea Pelzer, Andy Acia, Antoinette Contreras, Ashley Kate Adams, Bethany Hidden, Blithe Raines, Bryan Northup, Carmel Comendador, Carrie Erickson, Christi Ellington, Cody Devine, Connie Collier, Danielle Downs Spradlin, Dawn Hartman, Debbie Hartman-Otto, Debra Garnes, Dellina Pecor, Derick González, Desirae Hunter, Dina Faye Gilmore, Donna Cummings, Elizabeth Warren, Frankie Hernandez, Jackie Barnes, Jacqui Kriz, James Elden, Jamey Trotter, Jamin Barnes, Janet Milstein, Janne Kokkonen, Jasmine Moreno, Jason Barnes, Jennifer Carlson, Jennifer Hunt, Jessica Moreno, Jessica Murray, Johnny Ray, Kaycee Danielle, Kelly Lopez Shaw, Kelley Moreno, Kelly Hurtado, Kerry Crawford, Kimberly Faye Greenberg, Kruz Valero, Leah Aguilera, Leila Rogers, Linnea Lindh, Liz Jester,

Lucretia (Keshia) Whitmore-Govers, Máire Gardner, Marisa Villegas-Ramirez, Melita Ann Sagar, Michael Kushner, Michelle Harris, Mike Coste, Mindy Scranton-Morgan, Nancy Blanton, Nance Haxton, Nancy Nickle, Nataki Garrett Myers, Nea Herriott, Nick A. Moreno, Nita Manley, Patricia Dinsmore, Pedro G. Leos, Peter Giovanni, Rena Mason, René Rodríguez, Rob McCrea, Robert Esquivido, Robin Prather Ray, Robyn Colburn, Sabra Rahel, Sal Meza, Sami McNeil, Seth Scranton-Morgan, Shauna Merritt, Sloan Taylor Ledbetter, Stefani Deoul, Susan Madden, Tara Harbert, Terri Dean, Therease Logan, Trish DeBaun, Trisha Mendez, Todd Wylie, Vanessa Menendez, Warin Topunjasub, my colleagues at Red Rocks Community College, and the fantastic team at Cayélle Publishing. I am thankful to all my writing teachers for sharing their expertise with me, especially Francesca Lia Block. Thank you to Lea Schizas for making sure this novel happened. Every day I am grateful for the support of Edward Castillo Ortiz, my husband and partner in everything. And to the United Church of Christ for keeping me grounded and for helping me keep the faith. And, to my readers: thank you for letting me share my stories with you.

For My Grandmothers

ONE

An Original Composition

THE UNIVERSITY WAS two centuries old, a beacon of hope and a symbol of knowledge positioned on the highest hill of the sleepy town of Harmonville. The view from the third floor of the music building was one of a kind. From there, it was possible to not only see the entire town, but the three smaller towns surrounding it. Beyond that: the Pacific shoreline and sequoias.

In a large classroom with bare walls, November sunlight streamed in through the small windows, illuminating the otherwise dingy atmosphere with a warm, golden glow. Stadium-styled seats were occupied by undergraduate students, all filled with dimming aspirations to take their love of music and turn it into something tangible. The mood was somber and serious. Anxiety hung in the air like a misplaced chord.

Late and flustered, Sharleen Vega entered the room. The noisy entrance immediately killed the serious vibe. Strapped to her back was an overstuffed school backpack. It was black and blue, looking more like a bruised shell, a large hump that seemed intent on punishing her with pain for every step taken. The weight of it made walking a struggle. Finally, Sharleen made it to a seat. In the process of sitting, she accidentally smacked a fellow student in the head with her backpack.

Did I just hit poor Beverly with my backpack? Why am I such a mess today?

"Oh, sorry, Beverly," Sharleen said, tone genuine, voice warm and kind.

For a moment, other students appeared concerned blonde Beverly may have been knocked unconscious. Worry turned to relief when Beverly offered her classmates an enthusiastic thumbs up and gave the tambourine in her hand a light shake.

Standing near a piano was their professor, Lena Richter. She was formidable, German, and nearing retirement. She cleared her throat to command the attention of the room. At once, the students shifted their focus to her.

"Sharleen Vega, who always knows how to make a timely entrance, will be performing for us first today." The professor turned to Sharleen with a questioning stare. "And this is an original composition?"

Nervous, Sharleen stood, making her way through the sea of students until she joined her professor. One hand reached down and smoothed out invisible wrinkles in her skirt with damp palms.

"Yes, it is," she replied.

Sharleen sat down at the piano. Having put extra effort into her appearance for the occasion, her feet ached in the heeled shoes she wore. Her face felt hot. She now worried her makeup had melted into a sweaty mess. Feeling the eyes of her professor and classmates, she looked down at the keys.

"This is for my parents." Sharleen's whispered words were meant only for herself.

After a deep breath, Sharleen placed her fingers on the piano and played her song. A few notes in, the wrong key was struck. Embarrassed, she cringed.

"I'm sorry. May I start again?" she asked, avoiding the professor's eyes.

"Yes, you may," Professor Richter granted. "Without an apology in your words, or your notes this time."

Please let me get this right.

Sharleen performed the song with perfect execution. As usual, the students in the room were mesmerized, awed by her talent. Some looked envious as they watched Sharleen's fingers connect with the piano keys with seamless ease and fluid movements.

The song came to an end. That last note hung in the air, bittersweet and melodic. Professor Richter struggled to show no response but, in the end, couldn't help but look at Sharleen with a sense of pride. In similar fashion, the students applauded Sharleen's efforts. Beverly raised her tambourine and shook it vigorously until another student finally stopped the motion of her hand.

"The melody is haunting," noted Professor Richter. "The arrangement is superb. Your parents will be very moved. Have you played it for them?"

Sharleen swallowed the sudden wave of emotion rising in her throat. The mention of her parents always made her take pause; she needed a moment to keep composure intact and sadness at bay. "No," she replied. "but I know they heard it."

To Sharleen's surprise, Professor Richter approached. She leaned in as if to make certain her words were only heard by Sharleen. "May I see you in my office after class?"

Tensed, Sharleen held her professor's gaze. "Am I in trouble?"

"No," Lena replied with a slight shake of her head. "Not this time."

Filled with anticipation, Sharleen sat across from Professor Richter, who was poised behind the desk. The office was small but very organized. It was clear from the degrees on the walls and the awards displayed around the windowless room that Lena Richter was accomplished in her field. Sharleen stared at the accolades in awe as nerves dissolved into admiration.

On impulse, Sharleen reached toward the desk and helped herself to a few gumdrops, taking them from a green glass candy dish. Immediately she regretted the decision. The candy was chewy, very stale. She struggled to speak while gnawing away at the last bit of it.

"Professor Richter, I just want to start by saying how grateful I am," said Sharleen, still chewing. Panic struck, and she wondered if the obnoxious candy had caused her to drool in front of her favorite professor and unofficial mentor. "I know you recommended me for this scholarship. I wouldn't be able to finish the program next semester without it."

These things are horrible. I can't stop chewing. I will never eat gumdrops again.

The gray-haired professor projected a look of confusion and concern. "I'm so sorry, Sharleen," Lena said. "I didn't ask you to meet with me about your scholarship application."

Sharleen's cheeks burned with embarrassment by the sudden awkward moment. She stopped chewing, swallowed, and said, "You didn't?"

"No, the committee decided to give the scholarship to Beverly Schwartz." Lena slipped on a pair of reading glasses and glanced over handwritten notes on a yellow notepad. "Yes, they awarded it to Beverly last week."

"Beverly Schwartz?" Sharleen repeated, struggling to hide her shock and disdain. "She plays the tambourine. No offense, but is that even a real instrument?"

The professor's expression softened, as did her tone. "Sharleen, I asked you to meet with me because I'm afraid I have some difficult news to share with you."

At once, Sharleen gripped the wooden arms of the chair. "Is it about my song?" Was it that bad? You can tell me. I can take it."

It was rare to see Professor Richter smile, so Sharleen was surprised when a gentle one appeared on her face. But within a few seconds, it disappeared. "No. I'm rather impressed by your talents."

"Wow. Thank you. I'm impressed with yours, too."

"I know you've been working in our piano lab for a few semesters now," Lena continued. "Several students have mentioned you're a terrific tutor. In fact, I hear you're their favorite. I'm not surprised by this, at all."

Enthusiasm surged through Sharleen. It shone through her words, her eyes. "I love teaching. It's my thing, my passion," she explained. "Next to music, of course." Parched, Sharleen stopped. "By any chance, do you have any water in here?"

"No, sorry, I don't," Lena replied. "I'm sure you'll make a great teacher one day."

"I hope so."

The professor took a quick, deep breath before her next sentence. "Unfortunately, the university is making some budget cuts, and they have eliminated several part-time positions."

Already knowing the answer, Sharleen asked, "Is one of them mine?"

"Yes, I'm afraid it is. Moving forward, the piano lab will only be available by appointment and will be covered by one of our adjunct instructors."

Defeat carved through Sharleen's core like runes. Her posture went limp as if she were a balloon and the air keeping her alive was seeping out, and fast. "So, what you're saying is not only did the scholarship I needed go to someone else, but I also need to find a new job?" she said. "And figure out how I'm going to come up with the money to pay the remainder of my tuition. By January? Not to mention my rent."

A glimmer of empathy flashed in Lena's blue eyes.

"Yes, I would say that pretty much sums it up. That's exactly what you're dealing with."

Not wanting to hear another word, Sharleen stood to leave. "Great," she mumbled, and even though it was only November, she added, "Merry Christmas to me."

She stopped at the office door with a hand on the antique doorknob. "By the way," she announced, "those gumdrops are awful. Seriously, someone could lose a tooth eating those things."

The professor gave a slight nod in agreement. "I would assume they are. They were a gift when I started teaching here." She held Sharleen's stare. "Seven years ago."

Feeling she had nothing left to lose, Sharleen gave in to the held-back anger. "Well, you might consider throwing them out." Sharleen returned to the desk and picked up the candy dish. "Here. Let me save you the trouble." Holding the dish above a wastebasket, she flipped the container upside down. Gumdrops plopped into the trash in sticky clumps. A few stuck to the sides of the glass, so Sharleen gave the dish a few hard shakes. Finally, she returned the now-empty candy dish to its home on the professor's desk.

A second before she strolled out the door, their meeting ended with her final words on the matter, "Now, if you'll excuse me, I'm off to the computer lab to submit my resume and cover letter to anyone who's hiring. And apparently, I need to sign up for tambourine lessons, too."

TWO

Don't Worry About a Thing

SHARLEEN'S HARDSHIPS CONTINUED into the following week. Priding herself on being self-sufficient and resourceful, she felt confident that finding work would not be the struggle she thought it would be.

Deciding to register with a temp agency, they called the next morning with her first assignment: working in a call center. The job sounded simple, yet it was anything but. Overwhelmed by the complicated software system, her short-reaching headset, and the glaring eyes of a mean-faced boss named Polly who swam through the pool of employees like a stealthy shark, Sharleen knew her time there would be brief. It wasn't long before Polly stood beside Sharleen's claustrophobic cubicle, fuming in her nylons, orthopedic shoes, and polyester power suit. Without a word, Sharleen grabbed her cumbersome backpack and brown lunch bag, knowing she was fired. And she was.

On her way to the bus stop, a Help Wanted sign in the window of an all-night diner caught her attention. Desperate for help, the owner decided to overlook Sharleen's lack of restaurant work experience (she had none) and offered her a two-sizes-too-big waitress uniform, and a grease-stained printed schedule on the spot, along with the comment, "You're a very sad person. I can tell. See you tomorrow morning."

Optimistic, Sharleen tried her best as a waitress. Twenty minutes in, enthusiasm dimmed when she realized she'd served the wrong orders to the wrong customers. While attempting to fix the problem, she stumbled, dropping several plates in the process. They shattered into pieces on the grimy floor. As the angry owner stormed in her direction, Sharleen knew her fate was doomed. From behind the counter, she grabbed her overstuffed backpack and headed for the exit.

I am so totally fired. Again.

After scouring every online job posting out there, Sharleen eagerly accepted an offer to work for a neighborhood dog walking company, although she had never owned a dog in her life. Assuming dogs were less moody than people, Sharleen approached the new position with gusto. "Remember," the freckled-face owner named Tamara said in a voice that sounded like a Kindergarten teacher. "We are in control of the situation, the dogs are not. You are the human."

"I am the human," Sharleen repeated over and over as she struggled with five leashes and five dogs who were walking her, instead of she walking them.

As the local park came into view, Sharleen relaxed a little and let out a long sigh of relief. One of the dogs seized a lapse in Sharleen's state of alertness and broke free. She watched in terror as the beautiful dog headed toward the open door of an idling taxi with its designer leash trailing behind like a moving piece of evidence. An audible gasp escaped her lips when the dog jumped into the backseat of the cab. A well-intentioned stranger in an expensive-looking suit shut the car door. As the dog stared at Sharleen through the window, the taxi pulled away from the curb. Holding back a mixture of tears and profanity, Sharleen stood on the curb as the taxi and dog disappeared into the distance like a getaway car fleeing the police.

That afternoon, Sharleen sat at the table adjacent to her grandmother's shoebox of a kitchen. Defeat had left Sharleen's spirit crushed and her stomach empty. Alma Gutierrez, her grandmother, stood at the nearby stove stirring a pot of simmering beans.

Although in her late seventies, petite and quaint in appearance, Alma was a force to be reckoned with. The overpriced assisted living community she lived in was a constant source of anxiety because of the strict management. Her apartment was small and cramped, due in part to the impressive assortment of various forms of cows she collected—mostly porcelain. She dusted each piece every week on Thursdays, and washed them by hand on the first Saturday of every month.

"Don't worry about a thing, *m'ija*," she reassured Sharleen. "You're going to eat some dinner and then I'm going to write you a check."

Adamant, Sharleen shook her head. "No, you're not."

Alma gave her granddaughter a stern look. "You know better than to argue with me."

"I'm not arguing," Sharleen insisted. "I'm not taking money from you, *Lita*. You struggle enough as it is. I don't want you getting sick again."

Alma started to prepare a plate of food for Sharleen. She did so with the precision of a gourmet cook and with a deep sense of joy on her face which was damp from steam. "There's no need to worry about me," she said. "I have everything I need." Alma put the plate down in front of Sharleen. Then she was off to the kitchen again. Seconds later, she returned with a fork and a napkin.

Finally, Alma sat at the table with a cup of decaf coffee in hand. "It's not fair," she said. "How can they just take away your job like that?"

The sight and smells of the delicious food brought an immediate sense of comfort to Sharleen. Being with her grandmother always seemed to cheer her up—food or not—even on the worst days. "It was because of budget cuts," she explained before placing the napkin on her lap. "It happens."

"Taking money away from a school?" said Alma. "Are they crazy? Why would someone do that?"

"Don't worry. I'll figure something out," Sharleen said. "I always do."

"I want you to come see me more." It was a command. "That way at least I know you're not starving. You're too skinny, *m'ija*."

"I don't need a reason to come see you. I like being here with you."

Alma took a sip of coffee before she spoke again. "I worry about you. I don't like it … that you're on your own so much. Do you want another tortilla?"

"No, I'm fine," Sharleen said. "This is so much food.

"You need to eat more. I'll fix you some to go for later."

"You need to focus on your health."

Staring deep into Sharleen's eyes, Alma's gaze amplified tender sentiment. "You remind me so much of your mother. You look like her. You sound like her. I miss her every day."

Reaching out, Sharleen gave her grandmother's hand a gentle squeeze and said, "I know."

"I remember the night your mother came home after meeting your father for the first time. She was so young. Only sixteen."

Sharleen smiled. "I love this story."

"There was a wildfire in her eyes," Alma explained. "You have the same look when you talk about playing your piano. Your mother was so happy that night. I knew she was going to fall in love."

"I'm very glad they did," Sharleen said, followed by a short laugh. "Otherwise, I wouldn't be here."

"When your father came to our house to ask for your mother's hand in marriage, he was very nervous. But he was so polite. It was important to him to have our blessing," Alma recalled. "I can still remember their wedding like it was yesterday. So many flowers. So many people. All from the old neighborhood. They would be proud of you, *m'ija*. How hard you work. All that you do. How you look out for me."

Overcome by a wave of emotion, Sharleen put down her fork. "I would give anything to have them back. Even if for one day."

Alma stood. "That reminds me." She walked into the kitchen. "I have something for you."

From where she sat near the window, Sharleen watched as her grandmother reached into a kitchen drawer. From it, she took out something and held it to her heart before handing it to Sharleen. It was a strip of three pictures of her parents when they were young, taken in a photo booth years ago. Sharleen stared at their faces with a deep sense of longing. "I've never seen these pictures of them before," she said. "They look so happy ... and so young."

"It's yours now."

Sharleen couldn't take her eyes away from the photos. She swallowed, fighting back tears. "It's still so hard to be without them. Especially during the holidays."

"I know, *m'ija*."

"I hate it."

In her own tiny kitchen, Sharleen opened a can of soup, poured the contents into a pan on the stove, then clicked the burner on. Letting out a yawn, she stirred the thick mixture with a wooden spoon, realizing she was making the soup out of boredom, not hunger.

The kitchen table hummed with the buzzing of her cell phone. She leaned forward and reached for it. For the sake of space, only one chair was placed beside the small table, while the other three lived in the overflowing storage space in the basement of the apartment building. While the sole chair was practical, it was a constant reminder of how lonely she was. On the table, a small, lonely Christmas tree made its presence known with a half-eaten candy cane as its only decoration. Sharleen glanced at the sad tree with a mixture of pity and shame.

She placed the cell phone to her ear. "Hello?"

"Hello." It was a woman's voice, firm and authoritative. "May I speak to Sharleen Vega?"

Sharleen froze. Fearing the caller was another bill collector, she lowered her voice a few octaves, hoping if she disguised it the collector would end the call. "May I tell her who's calling, please?"

"My name is Maisy Prewett," the woman explained. "I'm a supervisor with the City of Harmonville's Department of Parks and Recreation."

It's a job. I can feel it in my bones.

"Let me see if Miss Vega is in. One moment, please." After a quick breath, Sharleen assumed her normal speaking voice, adding an extra layer of kindness to her words. "Hello. This is Sharleen."

"Sharleen, hello. My name is Maisy Prewett. I received your resume and application for a seasonal position at the Department of Parks and Recreation. Are you still interested?"

I was right!

Trying to contain her excitement, Sharleen struggled to keep her tone professional and calm. "Yes. Very much."

"I would like to invite you to my office for an interview," Maisy said. "Tomorrow at two o'clock?"

"I'll be in class until two-fifteen," Sharleen explained. "Would it be possible to meet at three?"

There was a pause before Maisy spoke again. "Yes, I can do that. Do you know where the Parks and Recreation department is located?"

"I do. It's the tallest building in town."

"Great. I look forward to seeing you then."

"Thank you for the call."

A newfound optimism hammered through her. It was a rush of hope, a surge of faith … a much-needed sense that everything was going to be all right.

To celebrate, Sharleen reached for the candy cane on the tree and started to eat it. On the stove, the soup boiled over. Leg muscles had her off the chair, rushing to the stove in no time at all to turn it off. In the process, the photo Alma gave her caught her eye from where it sat on the kitchen counter. Sharleen picked up the photo. Returning to the miniature Christmas tree, she placed the photo booth memory of her parents at the center, nestling it between two branches. Stepping back, it was a welcome sight of her two parents staring back at her, frozen forever in the trio of pictures.

For once, Sharleen felt the loneliness loosen its tight grip on her heart.

THREE

Never Late

*T*HE CITY BUS broke down in the middle of the busy street. It sputtered and coughed before it finally met its end. Panicked, Sharleen stood and gathered her things. She pushed the rear door open with both hands, barely able to squeeze through the tight space because of the width of her backpack. Finally, a frantic Sharleen exited the bus and hurried down the street, dodging people in the process like the stealth warrior of a video game.

Huffing and sweating, Sharleen entered the lobby of the five-story office building that housed the Parks and Recreation department. She spotted a bank of elevators and headed to the first one available.

A moment later, the elevator doors opened. She rushed down a long corridor toward the closed double doors of an office suite, catching other suite numbers in her peripheral vision while speed-walking. Before entering, she checked the suite number on a placard next to the door.

Maisy Prewett's office was simple, small, and cluttered. It was adorned with many trinkets that paid tribute to her Scottish heritage, including a coat of arms hanging on the wall. Sitting at the desk, her attention was directed to the large window behind her, which offered a view of the picturesque town square, including newly hung Christmas decorations. Maisy stared at them with a flash of nostalgia, an expression of sentiment that was rare for her to feel, or show.

This fifty-plus woman took gruff from no one. Life lessons. She had a large build, hair that was graying at the temples, and a permanent stress headache. Always dressed casually and for comfort, she wore her unofficial work uniform consisting of a Parks and Recreation embroidered Polo, khakis, and super comfy sneakers.

Turning away from the view, Maisy glanced at a clock on the wall. She then checked her wristwatch, as if needing a second opinion on time.

As if on cue, Sharleen entered the room with a burst of energy. The dark-haired, wide-eyed young lady appeared breathless and flushed. She struggled to slip her backpack off her shoulders before sitting down.

Leaning forward in the chair, Maisy was intrigued and impressed. It was clear Sharleen had made a considerable effort to be punctual.

"You must be Sharleen," Maisy began.

Taking in a deep, calming breath, Sharleen nodded.

"It's nice to meet you," said Maisy.

"Thank you." Tension around Sharleen's shoulders eased.

"I feel like I need to give you a moment to catch your breath."

Grateful for the mercy shown to her, Sharleen nodded and smiled. Within a few seconds, she explained her predicament. "The bus broke down. I ran the rest of the way. But I made it."

"I appreciate the effort you made to be here on time. Tardiness is one of my greatest pet peeves. What's yours?"

Sharleen opted for honesty and humor. "Not being able to breathe for one."

Although she didn't show it, Maisy was amused. "Tell me about yourself." she continued. "Why should I hire you?"

"I want to be a teacher," Sharleen explained. "A music teacher, to be exact. I'm in college. My last year."

"Yes, I see that here on your resume," Maisy noted. "I also see you grew up on the south side of town. That couldn't have been easy."

"Yes, I did," Sharleen replied. "And, no, it wasn't."

"That neighborhood still has its issues. It's a tough place to be."

"I wouldn't know," Sharleen offered. "I haven't been back there in seven years."

"That's a long time to be away from home, especially since it's so close."

For the first time in their conversation, Sharleen broke eye contact. "It's not really home for me anymore. It hasn't been for a while."

Sensing she'd tripped upon a sensitive subject, Maisy shifted the conversation away from the personal and back to the professional. "Your background in music is quite impressive." Without thinking, she added, "Your parents must be very proud of you."

Instant sadness filled Sharleen's eyes. "Unfortunately, I lost both of my parents when I was seventeen. They died in a house fire."

Cautious with her choice of words, Maisy said, "Oh, I'm sorry to hear that. Are they the reason you want to become a teacher?"

"It's all I've ever wanted to do. I know that teaching is my calling."

Maisy raised an eyebrow. "Despite the many challenges?"

Sharleen held Maisy's gaze. "I've never been afraid of a challenge," she said. "In fact, they only make me work harder."

"Yes, I get that impression," said Maisy. "You do realize this position is a temporary one. It's only for the holiday season."

Sharleen straightened her posture. Anticipation flashed across her face. "Yes, I do."

"And the pay isn't much."

"Some pay is better than no pay," Sharleen said with a grin. She followed this up with a more serious tone. "I really want the experience."

"And we show up even when the weather is bad."

"I have a warm coat," Sharleen insisted.

Maisy gave the young woman a stern look. "Can you direct a holiday variety show? Singing and dancing and funny skits, that sort of thing. Nothing fancy. And don't lie to me or tell me what I want to hear."

"Miss Prewett," Sharleen began, "I can direct the best holiday variety show this town has ever seen."

"That sounds pretty confident," said Maisy. "I like confidence." Maisy contemplated the decision to hire Sharleen. She displayed confidence, punctuality wouldn't be an issue if today's first meeting was any indication. Although hesitant, admiration won the battle. "I tell you what, Sharleen Vega. I want you to go down to the third floor to the human resources office. They'll have some paperwork for you to fill out, including a background check."

Sharleen stood with a rush of relief and joy. "That won't be a problem," she assured her new boss.

"We have a holiday staff meeting Friday morning at ten," Maisy instructed. "I expect you to be there. You'll find out what school you've been assigned to you then."

Sharleen nodded. "Thank you, Maisy."

Despite her cool front, Maisy couldn't help but crack a smile. "And you may call me Maisy."

"Thank you, Maisy," Sharleen repeated, followed by a short, awkward laugh. She grabbed her backpack and headed for the door.

"Oh, and another thing," Maisy said, stopping Sharleen in her tracks. "Don't be late," she warned. "Ever."

"I'm never late," Sharleen vowed.

Come Friday morning, a car alarm sounded, waking Sharleen from a deep slumber. She stirred and opened her eyes. The blinking clock caught her attention. The flashing numbers on the digital alarm clock on her makeshift nightstand, which consisted of two stacked milk crates, indicated a power outage occurred during the night.

At once, Sharleen sat up.

"Oh my God," she said, reaching for her cell phone. The screen read 9:40 a.m. Sharleen screamed in frustration. In a flurry, she scrambled out of bed and reached for the first pair of jeans she could find on the bedroom floor.

Hot and sweaty, Sharleen entered the large room, trying to remain unnoticed. The backpack made it tough to move without being detected, but she gave it her best effort. Passing by a long table, she grabbed a courtesy bottle of water sitting in an ice-filled pail. Her mouth was as dry as bone, and her throat ached from breathing so hard.

Sharleen did a quick scan, knowing that the people there were fellow staff members. Most looked like they were also college students.

In her usual casual attire, Maisy stood in front of the room behind a portable lectern. Behind her, the first slide of a presentation was projected on a screen. She spotted Sharleen's entrance and watched her move throughout the room.

Sharleen took a seat in the back row next to a young woman with a butterfly barrette in her long, blonde hair.

"Sharleen, I'm so happy you could join us," Maisy announced, with more than a tinge of sourness in her voice.

Everyone in the room turned in a wave of unison and stared at Sharleen.

Embarrassed, she stood, still holding the recently acquired bottle of water. "My apologies," she offered. "I had car trouble."

With a hand on her hip, Maisy shot Sharleen a look of disbelief and said, "Oh?"

Sharleen grinned and replied, "My trouble is I don't have a car."

The room erupted into laughter.

Why did I say that. What did I just do?

Maisy didn't appear amused. "I admire your entertainment skills," she said. "I hope you apply those when directing your holiday variety show."

"Yes," said Sharleen. "I definitely will."

She sat back down, uncapped the bottle of water, and took a few desperate gulps.

Looking out at the staff, Maisy said, "I'm so pleased that all of you are here. Working through the holidays is a real testament to your commitment to the youths in our town. So, thank you."

She then reached for a clipboard on a nearby table and glanced over the information on a piece of paper attached to it. "Now, I know you're all dying to find out what your assignments are for the next seven weeks, so let's get started."

The staff members leaned forward in their seats, anxious.

"First up, George and Cassie, you'll be working at the outdoor ice rink as ice guards."

The young woman sitting next to Sharleen mumbled, "I don't even know how to ice skate."

Smiling, Sharleen told her, "Better not tell Maisy that."

"Kimberly, you'll be joining them there as the concession stand manager," Maisy continued. "Hannah and Courtney, you've been assigned to coordinate the holiday bazaar at Tanglewood High School."

Two young women let out a simultaneous squeal of delight.

"Josh and Tammy, you've been assigned to coordinate the holiday parade."

Sharleen's new friend whispered to her, "They get the holiday parade every year."

"I can see why," Sharleen replied. "They look like they were born to ride a float."

"Now, for the holiday variety shows," Maisy said, with a hint of seriousness in her words. "I've hired three new program coordinators. First up, I need one of you three to volunteer to direct the show at Harmonville Elementary School."

Sharleen felt a ping of stress between her shoulder blades at the mention of the school. It was a familiar name.

"Where is that?" she heard someone ask.

"It's in the hood," said another voice in response.

Why do people call it that? It's just a place.

"I need someone who has a desire to work with at-risk youths," explained Maisy "These are children with complex lives."

The room remained quiet and still.

Seeming determined to appeal to the hearts of her staff, Maisy said, "There's never been a holiday program at that particular school, or any afterschool program, for that matter." She waited for a response. Instead, everyone avoided making eye contact with her, slinking down into their metal folding chairs, hoping to not be singled out by their boss. "Not in the history of this department," Maisy added. "Seriously, people, you have the chance to make a difference with this assignment. Does that matter to you?"

Sharleen waited and looked around the room for a response from someone, anyone. Finally, she couldn't take it anymore. With reluctance, she stood. All eyes shifted to her again.

"I'll do it," she announced.

Cassie tugged at Sharleen's sleeve in an attempt to pull her back down into the chair. "Are you crazy?"

Sharleen took a deep breath before addressing everyone in the room. "Those kids want to celebrate the holidays, too," she reminded them. "And I should know." She swallowed the wave of emotion creeping up her throat. *Please don't let me cry in front of these people.* "It's where I grew up." Sharleen then turned her focus to Maisy and said with conviction, "Send me to Harmonville, please."

Maisy offered a quick nod of approval. "Thank you, Sharleen. I look forward to seeing what magic you can make happen there."

Sharleen's cell phone buzzed. She pulled the phone out of her pocket, looked at the screen, and an immediate sense of dread filled her veins.

It was an incoming call from Harmonville Hospital.

Without hesitation, Sharleen grabbed her backpack, the empty bottle of water, and moved to the double doors, anxious to leave the room.

Maisy stopped her with her words. "Everything okay, Sharleen?"

Sharleen kept moving as she spoke. "I think something has happened to my grandmother," she said. "I'm sorry. I have to go."

FOUR

Fighting a Good Fight

*L*OST AND LUGGING her school backpack, Sharleen wandered down one corridor after another. The endless hallways felt like a cruel maze, leaving her overwhelmed and anxious.

I hate hospitals. Always have, always will.

Finally, she found her grandmother's room. Her name was written on a small dry erase board near the door.

Sharleen stepped inside, eyes adjusting to the dimly lit interior. Except for the steady beep of a heart monitor, it was quiet. Sharleen smiled at the sight of her grandmother. Alma was sitting up. She wore a light blue nightgown and her long silver hair was down. She looked up from the bible she was holding. It was the fancy one with the gold-trimmed pages, the one Alma only brought out on special occasions, or in a desperate moment.

"Hello, beautiful," she greeted. Sharleen knew her grandmother was weak. It was obvious when Alma attempted to smile but her mouth didn't move.

Sharleen crossed the room to be closer. She bent down and kissed her grandmother's cool-to-the-touch cheek. With one hand, she pulled a nearby chair closer to the side of the hospital bed and sat.

"What happened? Are you okay? Tell me everything."

"I'm fine," Alma said, but the slight tremble of fear in her voice gave her away. "I'm sure it's nothing serious. They just want to run some tests."

Sharleen's muscles tightened and ached. "What kind of tests?"

Alma lowered her gaze.

She's scared. She'll never admit it to me, but she's terrified.

"I don't know," Alma admitted. "And maybe I'm better off that way. What is it they always say … ignorance is bliss."

"If you won't tell me, I'll ask the doctor."

"I know you will," Alma said. "Whatever they tell you, ask for a second opinion."

"Who do I ask?"

Alma sighed. "I don't know … ask Jesus. He'll know whether it's my time to go or not."

"Please don't say things like that, *Lita*. You're all I have," said Sharleen. "You're my best friend."

Alma stared deep into Sharleen's dark eyes. "Something's happened," she decided. "Something is new. You haven't looked this happy in years."

"You're changing the subject," Sharleen said. "I got a job. And it's not awful."

"No dogs?"

Sharleen let out a small laugh. "No dogs."

"Oh, *m'ija*. That's wonderful. Tell me about it. It will be nice to hear some good news."

"Well, I'll be working as an afterschool program coordinator for the Department of Parks and Recreation. It's only part-time and it's just for the holidays."

Alma held up a finger stopping the conversation from moving forward before she made a declaration. "This will turn into something more," she insisted. "I feel it, *m'ija*. Something very important for you. Once they figure out how good you are, they won't let you go."

"Thank you, *Lita*. I hope so."

"Where will you be working?"

"Here's the strange part," said Sharleen. "I'll be working at Harmonville Elementary School. I volunteered. No one else wanted to do it."

Alma looked pleased. "This is good. It means you're going home," she said before closing the bible in her lap. "I always knew you would go back to the neighborhood someday."

"It will be strange to see it again."

"I remember your first piano recital there," said Alma. "You were so nervous but so talented. I wish I could do more for you, *m'ija*. I really do."

Sharleen reached for her grandmother's hand and squeezed it gently. "You already do too much. I just need you to feel better so we can spend Christmas together. I'm worried about you."

Alma ran her palm against the front of the bible as if the book was giving her some form of invisible strength. "I'm fighting a good fight," she said.

"You always do."

"Well, you know what us Gutierrezes are like," Alma reminded her. "Stubborn to the end."

Sharleen stood and went to the window. She pulled back the curtain and stared out at the night sky. "Have they told you when you get to go home yet?"

Alma lowered her voice to a secretive whisper. "No, but do me a favor and ask Dino. He's my favorite nurse," she confessed. "I think he's from Colombia."

Sharleen turned back to her grandmother with a giggle. "Have you been flirting with him again?"

Alma laughed, and the joyous sound of it filled Sharleen with a sense of much-needed relief. "Yes, but only because he lets me," Alma said. Her expression softened. "And at night, when no one else is around, he sings to me in Spanish."

As Sharleen left Alma's room, she nearly collided with the young-looking, attractive nurse, Dino, who possessed a boyish charm.

"Dino," she said, "I just want to say thank you."

His brows knitted together. "For what?"

"For being so nice to my grandmother," she said. "It means a lot."

"Alma is a special lady," Dino said. "I'm sure you're going to miss her a lot."

The world felt like it stopped. Sharleen stood, frozen in her steps. A river of sorrow poured through her and left her shaking. "Miss her?" she repeated. "Where is she going?"

The expression on Dino's face told Sharleen everything she needed to know—that her biggest fear was about to become a reality. "Sharleen, please forgive me," Dino said, nervous. "I thought … I thought you already talked to Alma's doctor. I'm so sorry."

"No, I haven't. Dino, what's going on?"

"You should talk to the doctor," he said. "Soon."

Sharleen scanned the hallway in both directions, searching for anyone who looked like a doctor.

"Well, where is she?" Sharleen demanded.

"At the moment, she's with other patients."

Sharleen moved to the first empty chair and planted herself in it. She gripped the arms of the chair, feeling a wild mixture of sorrow and rage. It pulsed in her hands and made her taut knuckles throb. "I'll wait," she said.

Dino gave a slight nod. "I'll let her know you're here."

The nurse turned to move down the hallway, but Sharleen stopped him with the urgency in her voice.

"Can you just tell me ... what did the tests say?" she said. "Please."

Dino took a deep breath before he replied. "You really should talk to the doctor. It's not my place to discuss this with you, as much as I want to."

"Please," Sharleen begged. "I just need to know." She stared into Dino's sad eyes as she began to cry. "Is the cancer back?"

FIVE

The Old Neighborhood

THE BUS ARRIVED at the stop. The door opened. Struggling, Sharleen managed to get through the opened door, barely able to fit through the exit because of the two overflowing book bags she carried, plus her backpack. Stepping onto the curb, she watched the bus pull away.

Sharleen remained still for a moment, taking in her surroundings. Familiar yet odd at the same time. She noticed the corner store, the neighborhood church, the empty park, and the Cuban coffee shop. All places she remembered frequenting as a child and a teenager.

Sharleen gave the four corners a second glance, trying to see the signs of the bad reputation the area had earned since she'd left. While the neighborhood was the oldest section of town, the alleged element of danger wasn't present.

It looks the same, but it doesn't feel the same.

Then a different notion came to mind.

Maybe it's me who's changed.

Sharleen began to walk, knowing her destination was only two blocks away.

As she approached the school, she smiled. The building itself was nondescript and looked like a gray box with a slanted roof, but there was a nostalgic quaintness to it that was appealing. Passing the chain-linked fence surrounding the adjacent playground, her enthusiasm waned. A sadness veiled the scenery. The playground primarily consisted of asphalt, a rusted set of swings, monkey bars, and a slide. All of the equipment had seen better days. And there was no grass in sight, only dead, golden weeds shooting up from cracks in the ground, desperate for sunshine or rain.

The wild mixture of emotions caused Sharleen to stop walking. Still staring through the fence, memories stirred.

I was the queen of chalk art, she remembered.

As if the memory were being reenacted in front of her, Sharleen saw a particular moment in vividness. She was seven. With a piece of chalk in hand, Sharleen was decorating the ground around her with her artistic version of the world. By the time her father arrived and watched from a distance, Sharleen had covered every inch of nearby space with planets, stars, and the moon. At the sound of her name, she looked up and saw her dark-haired father standing on the other side of the fence, smiling. She stood and ran to him, sliding her chalky fingertips through the metal links to touch his hands. As usual, they were oil-stained from the cars he worked on all day long.

Staring into her eyes, young Guillermo whispered to his daughter, "The world belongs to you, Sharleen. It's all yours."

"I love you, Daddy." Sharleen realized she'd said the words aloud, standing in the exact spot her father had stood seventeen years ago.

Shaking the memory off, Sharleen moved on. As she lumbered through the school parking lot, her bulkiness bumped into a few cars, setting off car alarms.

Relieved to have something to laugh at, she giggled and offered an apology to the cars. "Oops. My bad."

Continuing toward the main entrance, a rush of new emotions sprung forth, intense and sudden. Right before she entered the building, she glanced up to the top of the flagpole where the American flag waved hello, urging her to walk inside and take her first step on an unknown journey.

Sharleen entered the school, which was no easy feat considering all she carried. Inside, the building was comforting but worn. The overheated air emanated leftover scents from whatever lunch was served in the cafeteria earlier that day. After passing by a massive trophy case, Sharleen stopped and peered inside the first classroom. She smiled at the sight of engaged children sitting at miniature desks. It was the same classroom she once sat in as a Kindergartener.

Stepping into the main office, Sharleen approached the counter. Behind it stood Joyce McAllister, the dutiful and kind school secretary. She was an older woman with a gentle face, frosted hair, and a comforting presence.

"Hello," she said with a warm smile. "May I help you?"

"My name is Sharleen Vega. I'm from the Department of Parks and Recreation. I'm here to direct the holiday variety show and run the afterschool program," Sharleen explained.

Sentiment filled Joyce's eyes. The expression made Sharleen want to cry, but she kept her composure intact. "Sharleen?" Joyce said, staring. "Is that really you?" The woman reached for the glasses perched on top of her head and drew them down to her eyes. She gave Sharleen another look, which was more like a confirmation rather than an inspection. "Oh my, it is. I never forget a face. You might not remember me."

"I do," Sharleen assured her while fighting the temptation to reach across the counter and hug her. "You used to give me a popsicle whenever I was waiting to see the nurse. It's nice to see you again. It's been a while."

"I'm so glad you're back." A flicker of sadness flashed across Joyce's face. "I was so sorry to hear about your parents," she said, tone soft, filled with empathy. "It was a terrible tragedy."

"Thank you." Sharleen blinked back tears. "I miss them very much. It's a bit strange. Being back here, I mean. I feel like I've stepped back in time."

"Nothing much has changed," Joyce said. "This place is long overdue for a facelift, but you know how the school board is."

"Speaking of, I was told I need to check in with the principal."

"Yes, you do," said Joyce. "Her name is Betty Marchant. She's a lovely woman. We're very lucky to have her. But she's not available today. She's stuck in a meeting with the school board. I'll let her know you stopped by. I'll be in touch to reschedule your meeting with her."

"Thank you, Joyce." Sharleen moved to leave but stopped. "By the way, do you know where I'm supposed to go?"

"All of the students who signed up to be in the holiday variety show were told to report to the multipurpose room right after school."

Sharleen glanced up to the clock on the wall. "And when is that?"

In response to her question, a bell rang.

"I better hurry," she said. "I don't want to be late on my first day."

Sharleen entered the multipurpose room for the first time in twelve years, shocked by its appearance. The large room had long been forgotten. She stood near the double doors, hearing them click shut behind her.

The main focal point of the room was a raised stage built into the wall. Old-fashioned in style, the stage sat in silence, looking like it was waiting for ghosts from the vaudeville era to take center-stage and dazzle a long-ago audience. There were a few wooden steps on each side of the stage, allowing access up to the elevated performance area from the right or the left. Several stage lights were positioned from metal beams in the ceiling, aimed at the performance space.

One wall consisted of floor-to-ceiling windows facing the street outside. Sadly, the windows were covered by worn, dark drapes. The heavy material prevented any sunlight from entering the room.

This place feels like a gloomy cave. I remember it being bright and filled with joy. What happened?

Opposite the windows was a closed-off kitchen area that sat untouched. Sharleen remembered it was the area where lunch was served daily to a slow-moving line of tray-carrying grade school students. The majority of the room was still populated with cafeteria-style tables and bench seating, but even those looked decades old.

Sharleen moved to one of the tables and dropped her book bags on its surface with a soft thud. She slipped her backpack off and noticed how much her neck and back ached.

Her mood brightened when she approached an old upright piano, located near the stage. She played a few chords and winced in response.

Professor Richter would die on the spot if she heard how out of tune this thing is.

One of the double doors clicked open and someone entered. Sharleen turned to the sudden sound cutting through the eerie stillness and quiet.

An older woman with short-cropped hair, and a slight bend in her posture walked in, pushing a mobile shelf of books. She parked the cart near the stage. It was difficult to ignore that her simple outfit of faded jeans and a dark sweatshirt were accented by Christmas-themed accessories, including large, dangling earrings. It was clear she was a ray of holiday sunshine in an otherwise dark place.

Sharleen stepped forward, recognizing the woman at once. She was Willie Cole. Back then she'd been a firecracker, often leading the children into peals of laughter with her crazy but entertaining antics. Now, she looked long past retirement but still seemed somewhat spry and spirited.

Willie Cole looked up from her cart, and said, "You Sharleen?"

Oh no. She doesn't remember me. Do I look that different? My hair's much longer now and I'm definitely taller than I was when I was twelve, but not by much.

"Yes, I'm Sharleen."

Willie extended her hand to shake in a no-nonsense manner. "My name's Wilhelmina Cole," she said, "but most folks just call me Willie."

Sharleen shook the woman's hand. "It's nice to see you again, Willie."

The woman raised a suspicious eyebrow. "Oh? Have we met?"

Sharleen gestured to the musical instrument she was standing next to. "I was a student here about twelve years ago," she explained. "I played the piano. A lot."

Willie leaned in for a closer look at Sharleen before saying, "I remember you. You *did* play the piano. And you were good, too.

You came all the way back here to direct a variety show? You're either desperate for a job or way too generous for your own good."

Sharleen smiled. "Probably a little bit of both. I'm working for the Department of Parks and Recreation. Just for the holidays. I'm in college. My last year. And this is the fourth job I've had in the last two weeks, not by choice."

Willie appeared skeptical. "But you don't live around here anymore, do you?"

"No, I moved after my ... I moved to be closer to school," Sharleen said. "And my grandmother. She lives in an assisted living building a few blocks away from my apartment. But I still live in Harmonville. Different neighborhood, but the same town."

Willie made a sound that was loud and sounded like *ha!* "Different?" she said. "You're not lying. I'm surprised this school stays open, to tell you the truth."

"Oh, no. Are things that bad?"

"Since it's your first day and all, I'll spare you the sad details."

"I'm very happy to be here," said Sharleen. "I've never directed a holiday show before, but it should be fun. I'm looking forward to working with the students."

Willie chortled and said, "Yeah ... good luck with that."

The doors of the multipurpose room flung open as if they were being ripped from the hinges. Willie and Sharleen were invaded with students rushing in, all anxious, all chatting, all curious.

Surprised by the huge turnout, Sharleen quickly made her way to the stage. She scrambled up the mini staircase and positioned herself downstage center. She looked out at the crowd looking up at her.

"Hello, everybody," she said. "Wow, there's a lot of you here." A quick head count indicated there were at least thirty students.

She stared at their young faces and paused for a moment, over-whelmed by the beautiful sight.

A young girl stepped forward, looking up at Sharleen. Her eyes reflected awe and reverence. Sharleen estimated she was around ten years old, maybe a little younger. Long, light brown hair was pulled back into a single braid. "Are you the director?" the student asked.

"I am," Sharleen replied with a nod. "My name is Sharleen Vega. You may call me Miss Sharleen."

A young boy approached and stood next to the girl. Sharleen sensed they were the same age and possibly related, although his features were darker. He didn't look impressed. "Are you another teacher?"

Still smiling, Sharleen answered with, "Maybe someday, but for now I'm an afterschool program coordinator. What I'd like for you to do is line up over here." Sharleen gestured to the bottom of the staircase on the left side of the stage, the one closest to the piano. "We have a lot of work to do in order to put this show together. I'm going to need all of your help."

"What kind of a show is it?" the unimpressed boy asked.

"It's a holiday variety show," Sharleen explained.

The girl raised her hand. "Do we get to sing?"

"What about dancing?" the boy inquired. "Do we get to dance?"

"Yes and yes," Sharleen replied. "One at a time, I would like for each of you to come up here and introduce yourselves. Since we're going to be working together, I'd like to know who you are."

The young girl put her hand up again. Sharleen was already impressed by how polite she was for someone so young. "Would it be okay if we get our library books first?" she asked, with a slight tremble in her voice. She looked nervous, which only made her more endearing to Sharleen. "Willie only brings us books once a month and the good ones go fast."

Sharleen looked to Willie for guidance. In response, the older woman offered a slight nod of approval, like a pitcher communicating with an umpire.

Sharleen moved to the mini staircase and walked down the steps. She joined Willie who was standing next to the mobile book cart, guarding it from anxious hands. "Are you the school library?"

"The portable one, yes," Willie said. "The district won't give us the money to build a new one after the last one was condemned."

There was no question in Sharleen's mind. Introductions and rehearsals could wait. She turned to the students and announced, "Yes, please get your library books first. And then we can start."

As if an invisible barricade had dissolved, the students made a mad dash to Willie, overwhelming her. On instinct, Sharleen jumped in to help.

"I've never seen so many young people so happy to have books to read," Sharleen said to Willie. "You would think we were giving away free cell phones or video games."

Willie gave her a look. "I know you've been away for a while but try to remember how happy you were to have something new."

A few minutes later, Sharleen sat at the piano with her fingers poised above the keys. About a dozen students were standing in a short line, waiting their turn. The other students were sitting at tables talking or reading.

Willie was nearby, mopping the floor with something that smelled like pine trees.

As each student reached the first of the line, Sharleen worked with them on scales, trying to determine their singing ability.

I'm in trouble. Very few can carry a tune.

Then, the polite young girl stepped up to the piano.

Poor thing. She's terrified.

She leaned in close to Sharleen and whispered in a shaky voice, "Do I have to sing in front of everyone?"

Another girl who was taller and bigger stepped forward. Short curly hair bounced with every step. "Hurry up, Ivy," she said. "The rest of us want a turn, too."

The impatient girl had a redheaded sidekick who was smaller and mouse-like. She stood next to the ringleader with a threatening smirk on her face. "She won't sing," she explained to Sharleen with a dramatic hand on her tiny hip. "She never does."

The bigger girl spoke again. "You're wasting your time, Miss Sharleen," she said. "She refuses to sing in front of anyone."

Ivy looked as if she were on the verge of tears. Sharleen gestured for her to come closer so their conversation was out of earshot of the other girls.

"What do you say I let these two girls go next and then everyone can leave except for you and me?" she offered. "Will you sing then?"

Ivy gave this some thought before nodding in response and agreeing to the terms. "Yes, but not in front of them. Not ever," she vowed. "I'm sure you can tell … but Raquel and Camilla don't like me."

Moments later, all the students were gone except for Ivy.

At the piano, Sharleen started the scales.

Young Ivy took a breath and began to sing.

Sharleen continued to play with an invigorated enthusiasm, inspired by Ivy's beautiful tones.

Her pitch is perfect and her voice is remarkable.

With her focus on Ivy and the piano, Sharleen was unaware that a man had entered the room. When she finally noticed him, he remained in the back in silence, listening to Ivy sing. An expression of pride on his face.

Who's that? And how can we be introduced?

Sharleen stopped playing. The final note disappeared up into the ceiling. She turned to Ivy and with a rush of excitement said, "You have a very beautiful voice."

Ivy blushed, embarrassed by the recognition of her secret talent. "Thank you," she said, with her green eyes cast to the freshly mopped floor.

"Tell me your name again," Sharleen prompted.

The man approached the piano, and in doing so Sharleen's suspicions were confirmed: he was even more handsome up close. He looked to be in his early thirties. He possessed a combination of rugged good looks and an athletic build. From the clothes he wore, she guessed he did manual work for a living, maybe construction.

He must be her father.

"Her name is Ivy," he answered.

Sharleen stood. "And you are?"

"Jake Arlington," he said. "Her father."

I was right and, oh my God, look at his eyes.

"It's nice to meet you. You must be very proud of your daughter," Sharleen said. "Her voice ... it's very strong. Has she been taking singing lessons for a long time?"

Jake gave her a strange look. "No time for lessons, I'm afraid," he said, sounding brisk. "Ivy, get your things. Time to go."

Sharleen moved in his direction. "We'll only be a few more minutes. I would love to work with her until five, if that's okay. You're welcome to stay and watch. Ten more minutes?"

"Sorry," he said. "We have a lot going on right now."

"But she'll be back? Tomorrow?"

Jake was already heading for the exit, with his daughter following close behind clutching her library books, a lunch bag, and a sweater.

"You'll have to ask her," Jake said before leaving the room.

Ivy tossed her words over her shoulder, still moving, still trying to keep up with her father. "I'll be back, Miss Sharleen." Her words sounded like a promise.

"It was nice to meet you." Father and daughter already gone. Sharleen sat back down at the piano. "Both of you."

SIX

The Principal's Office

ALMA WAS RESTING but stirred when she realized Sharleen was seated at her bedside. She struggled to reposition herself to get a better look at her granddaughter.

Sharleen remained pensive. The conversation she'd just had with Alma's doctor all but sealed Alma's fate.

It's just a matter of time, I'm afraid. We'll do everything we can to keep her comfortable.

The thought of losing her last living relative was too much to bear. Alma's death would be a grief too strong to survive.

What am I going to do without her?

"Sharleen?" Alma's concern was heavy in her voice. "What's the matter?"

Forcing a smile, Sharleen knew better than to cause more worry. Her grandmother needed as little stress as possible. "Just tired," she answered.

Alma reached out and gave the top of Sharleen's hand a few gentle pats. "I want to hear all about your first day. How was it?"

"Never mind about me. It's you I'm worried about."

"Me? Why worry about me? I'm an old woman who has lived a wonderful life. I'm fine, *m'ija*."

Sharleen felt the first tear fall. "I'm so scared of losing you."

Alma let out a long breath. "I know," she said. "It's just been the two of us for the last seven years."

"And they've been wonderful years," Sharleen said. "You're my best friend, *Lita*."

"I don't want you to be alone." Alma's tone had taken a stern turn. "I hope you find love in this world. I wish that for you. I want you to find somebody."

Not wanting her grandmother to see her cry, Sharleen stood and went to the window. Outside, night had arrived. Somewhere in the far distance, Sharleen could make out a string of holiday lights blinking. "Is it possible to feel love in more than one way?" she said. "I understand what it means to love a person, but can you also love doing something more than love anyone?"

By the time Sharleen got home, the hour was late. Although she had no appetite, she prepared dinner, which consisted of microwaved leftovers she dug out of the almost bare refrigerator. For the first time in months, she thought about reaching out to her childhood friend Ruby, but then decided against it, remembering they hadn't spoke for a couple of years. Since Ruby left town to attend college on the other side of the country.

Instead, Sharleen ate in silence, sitting at the table for one in the sliver of a space next to the kitchenette. The sound of her fork on the plate seemed to echo and accentuate the fact that she was alone.

After a few bites, she shoved the plate away. The loneliness unbearable. And never-ending. Attention was drawn to the Christmas tree sitting on the kitchen table, just a few inches away from the half-eaten dinner. Sharleen reached out to the trio of photos of her parents when they were young, touching their faces with a gentle fingertip.

And then she cried.

The next afternoon, Sharleen entered the school office and approached the main counter.

Joyce was sitting at her desk, sipping a cup of tea. She stood when she saw Sharleen.

"Everything okay?"

"Yes, of course," Sharleen answered.

Joyce let out a sigh of relief. "For a moment I was worried you were here to tell me you were quitting."

Sharleen leaned closer. "Does that happen a lot around here?"

Joyce's warm smile turned upside down into a sad pout. "I don't even bother ordering name tags anymore."

Sharleen reached into one of her book bags and retrieved an event flyer, something she had designed less than two hours ago at the university's computer lab. She placed it on the counter. Joyce glanced at it. She turned her head as if she were trying to read it upside down. To help her, Sharleen flipped the paper around.

"I was just wondering … I designed this flyer for the holiday show," she said. "Is it possible to get copies made so I can hand them out? I'm sure some of the parents would like one."

Two people entered the office. One was a beautiful brunette who glanced Sharleen up and down before offering an arrogant smirk and a judgmental look of disapproval. The thin-haired man was very fashionable and stared intently at the woman, with a fan-like devotion in his bright, wide eyes.

"I would love to," Joyce said, "but our copy machine hasn't worked in a couple of months. It's on my list of things to get fixed though."

"Oh … I see," said Sharleen. "I'll see what I can do, then. Thanks, Joyce."

"You're welcome. For what it's worth, I'm glad you aren't quitting."

Sharleen moved to leave, but the scowling woman blocked her path.

Is she the rude wicked witch of the school?

"Quitting?" she said with a sneer. "Already? My, my."

"I'm not actually," Sharleen explained. "I have no plans to quit … now or ever."

"Really?" Those two syllables were stretched out, sounding like a mean purr. "I don't believe we've met. I'm Holly."

The baby-faced man stepped forward and said with enthusiasm, "I'm George." He looked curious. A bit dopey, but friendly.

"Sharleen Vega." She said, taking a closer look at Holly. "I'm sorry I keep staring, but you look so familiar. I feel like I know you."

Holly let out a short laugh, sounding like an evil wind-up doll. "What a small world. We went to school together, Sharleen. Right here. Don't you remember?"

"We did?" Then, it hit her. Sharleen knew exactly who Holly was. She was someone she'd been trying to forget for years. "Oh, we did. I remember you, Holly. You look different now. Older," she said. "You were awful to me."

Holly let out a mini gasp. "That's all in the past now. We're grownups." George was leaning in too close for Holly's comfort, like a zealous dog hoping for a few pats on the head. Holly gave him a stern look and he retreated. "So…" she continued, "I hear you've been sent here to direct a Christmas pageant. Is that it? That sounds … fun."

"Are you a teacher here?" Sharleen asked, fearing the answer.

"I am," replied Holly, and it was clear she was proud of this fact. "For two years now. Fourth grade. They're monsters but they love me."

"Holly is everyone's favorite teacher," George interjected. "Just ask Joyce."

Sharleen looked to Joyce for confirmation. It was obvious the school secretary was struggling to maintain a polite façade. "Everyone is entitled to their own opinion," she stated.

In response to her neutral answer, Holly shot Joyce a death stare. She then turned her attention back to Sharleen. "I can't wait to come and see your little show. I'm always up for a good laugh." She moved to leave, expecting George to follow, but he was too busy grinning at Sharleen like a lovesick fool. "Come along, George!" Holly snapped. "I have some erasers for you to clean."

On command, George hurried off, rushing to catch up with a fast-moving Holly storming down the hallway like a nightmare in heels.

Sharleen turned to Joyce and said with a gentle smile, "Like you said … nothing much has changed."

On stage, Sharleen was teaching the students the steps to the opening number. For the most part, she noticed they were engaged and enthused, except for Raquel and Camilla who were busy making faces at Ivy, who was doing her best to ignore them.

Standing and watching them run through the first eight counts, Sharleen admired how quick Victor was with learning the choreography. He was a natural dancer; the steps came to him with ease.

"Very nice job," she said to him.

He beamed in response to the praise. "Thank you, Miss Sharleen."

"Okay, everyone!" she announced. "That's all for today. I'll see you back here tomorrow."

The students started to gather their things and leave, except for Ivy. She sat at a table. Sharleen assumed she was waiting for her father to arrive, as was she—secretly.

"Bye, Silent Ivy," taunted round-faced Raquel as she snaked her way out of the multipurpose room.

"Poor baby," rail-thin Camilla added. "Silent Ivy doesn't wanna sing."

"Leave me alone," said Ivy.

Sharleen struggled with the impulse to run after both girls, drag them back into the room by their hair, and make them apologize to Ivy, who had more talent than both girls combined.

Instead, she helped Victor slip his backpack on, knowing firsthand what that struggle was like. "I meant what I said earlier," she told him. "You're a really good dancer."

"Thanks," he said. "I like dancing a lot but..."

"But what?" she prompted.

"But some people make fun of me for it." His dark brown eyes cast to the ground.

Sharleen sat on the bench seat so she and Victor could be eye to eye. "The other students?"

Victor nodded. Sharleen wanted to hug him. "Yeah ... and my dad," he said. "He doesn't let me dance at home anymore."

Sharleen swallowed her emotions, knowing that if she didn't, she'd be crying her eyes out in front of Ivy, Victor, and Willie within seconds. "Well, when you're here with me I want you to dance as much as you want," she said. Sharleen glanced over to where Willie was watching her from a distance while she mopped the always-dirty floor. She offered Sharleen a reassuring smile.

Jake entered the room with car keys in hand. He looked in Sharleen's direction before checking his watch.

While Ivy seemed happy to see her father, Sharleen noticed her reluctance to leave rehearsal.

"C'mon, Ivy," Jake urged. "Time to go."

Ivy stood and offered her father a pouty frown. "Already?"

Sharleen approached Jake. It was then she noticed his dimples. "It's nice to see you again, Mr. Arlington. I don't think we were properly introduced last time. My name is Sharleen Vega."

"I know who you are," he replied with curtness in his words. "You're the new teacher."

Despite his impatient and somewhat irritated tone, Sharleen continued to smile. "I'm not exactly a teacher … yet."

He gave her a look and she noticed how dark and intense his eyes were. Like they could see right through her. "Oh? What are you then?"

Ivy moved and stood between them. "I already told you. She's our director. For the Christmas show."

At the sound of his daughter's voice, Jake's demeanor softened. "This show is all she talks about at home," he explained.

"I hope that's a good thing," said Sharleen.

"Yeah … it's been a good distraction for her."

"I do hope you come and see it … the show, I mean."

He looked at his watch again. "When is it?"

On impulse, Sharleen reached into her book bag and pulled out the flyer—the only copy she had. Without hesitation, she handed it to Jake.

"Well, I just happen to have a flyer right here. Just for you, Mr. Arlington."

He took the flyer with a sense of obligation, not interest. "Thank you, Christine."

"It's Sharleen," she corrected.

"Yes, right. Sorry about that."

Sure, you are. If you weren't so damn handsome, I'd give you a piece of my mind, even in front of Ivy and Willie.

Jake started to leave but suddenly stopped. He looked back. He seemed to be staring at Ivy and Sharleen, standing together side by side. For a brief second, Sharleen swore she saw a flash of tenderness appear on his beautiful face. Then, just like that, it was gone.

Did I just imagine that?

To confirm she hadn't hallucinated his kinder side, he said, "It's nice to meet you, too." And she believed him. He followed this up with, "Call me Jake."

For a moment, Sharleen felt she was back in the fifth grade, smiling at a boy she had a crush on who hadn't noticed her until the last day of school. "Alright, Jake," she replied.

"I'll be here … for the show."

With that, Jake and Ivy were gone.

Within seconds, a well-dressed formidable black woman who looked to be in her fifties appeared in the double doorway of the room. She looked authoritative and important.

"You must be Sharleen." Her tone was warm but firm.

"I am."

"I'm Betty Marchant, the principal of this school," she explained. "Can you stop by my office before you leave for the day?"

"Yes, of course."

"Thank you."

Betty disappeared just as quickly as she appeared.

Looking concerned, Victor moved to where Sharleen stood next to the section of cafeteria tables.

"Miss Sharleen," he said, "are you in trouble?"

Sharleen let out a sigh. "Probably, Victor. I usually am."

"Yeah," he said with a grin. "Me, too."

Not too long after, Sharleen walked into Betty's office and sat, struggling to maneuver her backpack and stuffed book bags.

Betty looked up from her computer screen and shifted her attention.

With a secret smile, Sharleen noticed a candy dish filled with jellybeans on Betty's desk. She glanced around. The office was colorful and vibrant. Students' artwork displayed everywhere.

Betty cleared her throat. "Miss Vega, thank you for stopping by."

"Thank you for the invitation," she said. "Joyce mentioned how busy you are. It's so great to finally meet you."

"Likewise. Meetings and phone calls keep me from the thing I love the most."

"Vacation?" cracked Sharleen. Instantly she regretted her word choice as soon it was out of her mouth.

Betty seemed unfazed. "Spending time with my students," she said.

"They're very talented," Sharleen gushed. "Really, some of them should be in a performing arts school or taking lessons from professionals."

"Yes, about that," said Betty. "How confident are you in their ability to perform? And be honest."

"It sounds like you're looking for some type of guarantee."

"I am. It's no secret that our school has seen better days. I keep asking for help, but I'm not getting any," said Betty. "I'm at the end of my rope, but I have a feeling with you around, we might just be able to hang on."

"I appreciate your confidence in me, especially since I just started here," she said. "Honestly, it hasn't changed much since the sixth grade."

Betty raised an eyebrow. "You were one of our students?"

"I was. I spent seven long years here," Sharleen said. "Most of them were wonderful. Except for Holly. No offense, but did you really have to hire her?"

"I had no idea," said Betty. "That you were a student here, I mean. Then you must realize how much we need your help."

Sharleen leaned forward.

You have my full attention, Betty Marchant.

"I'm listening," she said.

"Unfortunately, it all has to do with funding."

"Doesn't everything?"

"Yes, I'm afraid so," said Betty. "I've been fighting with the school board every day since I took this job."

"And you need some backup?" Sharleen asked. "Say no more."

Betty stood and came around the desk. She gazed intently at Sharleen. "I need you to put together the best holiday show this town has ever seen. If you can do that, I will invite the superintendent to the performance. Jessica owes me many favors, and it's time to collect."

"What does the show have to do with it?"

"Among other things, I want our school to have a performing arts program," Betty explained. "A funded program. There's nothing like that for young people in this area. I need the super-intendent to come here and see the show and meet the students."

"And give you more money?"

Betty nodded. "Something like that. I don't want to say it, but this program and the show are our last hope…"

"You might not want to say it, but is it the truth?" Sharleen asked.

Betty took a deep breath. It was then Sharleen noticed the exhaustion in the woman's eyes. "I'm afraid they might shut us down," she said, already sounding defeated. "When you look at our test scores and then at the funding they give us to survive on … it's not a winning combination."

In response to this, Sharleen helped herself to a handful of jel-lybeans.

"I'm sorry," she explained. "I'm a nervous eater."

"Please … help yourself. That's what they're here for," Betty said. Then, she added, "I buy a new bag every week."

And for that reason alone, I will put my heart and soul into this.

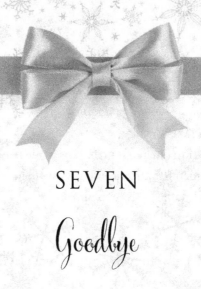

SEVEN

Goodbye

AFTER HER MEETING with Betty, Sharleen exited the building with her backpack and bookbags in tow. Outside, the November sun was starting to set. There was a crisp chill in the air. To her surprise, Jake was parked in a red pick-up truck near the entrance, under the bare branches of a cluster of redwood trees. Sharleen turned, hearing someone behind her. Ivy emerged from the school holding a library book.

"I got it!" she shouted to her father.

The second Ivy saw Sharleen, she stopped. Without hesitation, Ivy took her by the hand and lead her in the direction of Jake's truck.

"Ivy," Sharleen said, only half-protesting. "What are you doing?"

And is your father single or divorced or what?

"Miss Sharleen, come say hi to my dad again," Ivy insisted. "He smiles when he talks about you."

He does, does he?

As they reached the truck, Jake rolled his window down.

Why do I suddenly feel very awkward? His eyes, though ... and he's smiling at me. Damn. I'm doomed.

"Still here?" Jake asked.

Sharleen couldn't help but grin. Jake made her giddy, a feeling she couldn't remember anyone else stirring in her. "I had to report to the principal's office," she explained.

"I hope they didn't fire you."

"No, not yet."

The moment between them shifted from playful to odd when neither of them knew what to say next.

I can't just stand here staring at him like a deranged lovesick stalker.

"Well ... I have a bus to catch," Sharleen said, ending the strangeness. "Have a great night."

Sharleen started to walk in the direction of the bus stop, thankful the evening air was cool enough to calm the hot flush warming her face.

Jake jumped out of his truck and joined her. They walked for a few steps before Sharleen stopped and turned to him.

"Are you walking me there?" she asked. "Really, you don't have to. It's only two blocks."

"You take the bus?" he said. "Carrying all that stuff? And what is all of this? You're too young to be a bag lady. Do you run away from home every day?"

"I have a lot to carry," she explained. "And the bus isn't so bad."

"No," he said, still smiling. "I can't let you do this."

"Do what? Walk to the bus stop? I do it all the time."

He touched the sleeve of her sweatshirt. "Let me give you a ride home."

I would love nothing more.

Sharleen used the moment to take a quick look into Jake's dark eyes. "Are you sure?"

"You're Ivy's favorite teacher," he replied. "It's the least I can do."

I'm not a teacher yet but I'm not going to argue the point with you because you're so damn hot, and I'm actually sick of taking the bus. So, there.

"Thank you, Jake. I appreciate it."

They returned to the pick-up truck, where Ivy welcomed them with an adorable giggle.

"Do you want me to sit in the back?" Sharleen asked.

"In the back of the truck?" Jake looked and sounded confused. "You'll freeze to death."

"I don't mind. Fresh air and all that."

Stop it, Sharleen. You sound like a lunatic.

"No, silly. You can sit up front," he said. "With me. Where it's warm."

"Okay. If you insist."

Sharleen climbed into the truck and sat next to Ivy, who was wedged between them.

As soon as Sharleen was settled in and buckled up, Ivy tapped on her arm, leaned in and whispered, "We can trade places. If you want to sit closer to my dad. I don't mind."

She's the cutest thing ever.

"I think I'm good here, thanks," Sharleen whispered back.

Jake was now behind the steering wheel. He turned to Sharleen and asked, "Where to?"

A half hour later, Sharleen unlocked the front door, stepped inside, and dropped her belongings on the apartment's hardwood floor.

Immediately, she went to the miniature Christmas tree on her kitchen table. She looked at her parents' picture.

"I think I'm in trouble," she said to their photographed faces. "Big trouble. He walked me to the door. And he isn't married."

Her cell phone buzzed. Sensing something was wrong, she reached into her pocket to retrieve it.

"Hello? … This is her…" Sharleen felt air leave her body as if someone had punched her in the stomach. The room started to spin. "Thank you for letting me know." Already there were tears. "I'll be right there."

When Sharleen entered the hospital room, Dino was standing beside Alma's bed. His expression was one of immense sorrow. Sharleen knew bad news was coming, the news she'd been dreading.

Look at her. She's just sleeping. She's tired, but okay.

Then, Dino spoke and his warm voice killed any hope Sharleen was clinging to. "Sharleen," he said. "I'm so sorry."

Sharleen crept closer. "*Lita?*"

Dino took a deep breath and then spoke again. "She passed away a few minutes ago," he explained. "She's not suffering anymore."

Numb, Sharleen went to her grandmother. She wiped the tears from her face before she bent down to kiss her cheek.

Overwhelmed with grief, it was difficult to get the words out, but Sharleen tried. "What am I going to do?" she said. "I just lost my best friend."

She felt Dino's hand on her shoulder. It was gentle and light, like the falling feather from the wing of an angel. "Is there someone else I should call?"

Sharleen wiped her face with her sleeve. "No … we didn't have anybody else. Just each other. Just the two of us."

"Speaking of…" Dino opened a drawer in the nightstand next to Alma's bed. He reached inside and pulled out a small white velvet box. He handed it to Sharleen. "A few days ago your grandmother gave me very specific instructions. She said I was to give this to you … when she went. She said you would know what it was. She made it very clear she wanted you to have it."

Sharleen stared at the soft object in her hand. "Thank you."

"I know you'll miss her very much."

Sobbing, Sharleen welcomed an offered hug from Dino. After, she moved away from him and fell into the chair next to Alma's bed, exhausted from sadness and the day.

"Do you mind if I sit here for a few minutes with her?" she asked.

Dino offered a kind smile and said, "Take your time. I'll be down the hall if you need anything." He turned and left the room.

The sudden hush that followed felt strange and cruel. The room seemed dark and shrouded in suffocating sadness.

My heart is broken. You can't leave me.

Sharleen clutched the box in her hands as tears continued to tumble.

"*Lita*, what am I going to do without you here?" She stared at her grandmother, wishing this was all a big mistake. That she'd wake up any second now. "I don't even know how to say goodbye to you."

EIGHT

A Smile

MAISY LOOKED UP when Sharleen entered her office. From the strange expression on her face, Sharleen couldn't tell if Maisy was startled, surprised, or both. Sharleen sat, landing in a chair with a thud. For once, she was empty-handed—no backpack and no book bags.

What am I doing here? This was a bad idea. She's looking at me like I'm insane. Because I probably am.

"Everything okay?" Maisy asked. "No offense, but you look like hell."

Sharleen opened her hands and stared at her palms, studying them, hoping that words would magically appear on her skin.

I knew exactly what I wanted to say when I was on the bus. Now that I'm here, I feel dumb.

"After I leave here, I have to go to my grandmother's apartment and decide what to do with her belongings ... because she died last night." Numb. That's how she felt saying those words out loud.

Silence followed. Maisy's office felt motionless like it was a scene from a movie and someone had pushed the pause button.

Finally, Maisy stood and went to her. She put a comforting hand on her shoulder. "Sharleen, I'm so sorry."

"Thank you." Sharleen managed to give Maisy a faint smile, but the effort to do so was tiring. "On the bus ride over here, I kept thinking about how I would get my words right when I saw you ... how I'm going to tell you."

Maisy leaned in. "Tell me what?"

Sharleen dropped her gaze. "I can't work at the school anymore," she said. "I'm wondering if you could find me another assignment and send me somewhere else. Anywhere else."

Maisy folded her arms across her chest. "I don't understand. Why do you want to leave? The principal has been raving about you. She called me yesterday and told me you were the best thing to happen to her students in years. And I believe her."

Don't cry. Even though Maisy is saying nice things to you and you thought she hated you, don't fall apart. Not here. Not now.

Inhaling long, deep calming breaths to halt the trembling reverberating through her body, Sharleen said, "Every day when I get off the bus and I walk to the school, I have to pass by my old house," she explained, hearing the teeter in her own voice. The tears were threatening to break free at any second. "But because of the fire it looks so different now, I barely recognize it. The only thing that hasn't changed is the address. It's where I grew up. It's the last place I remember seeing my parents alive." She took another breath. Her body was weak with exhaustion. "There's too many memories."

Maisy moved back to her desk and sat. She reached for a coffee cup, took a sip, and then said, "You want to quit because of sad memories?"

Sharleen nodded. "Yes, I do," she said. "Also … the principal told me … about the budget issues. How important this holiday show is to them. I can't let them down. I can't ruin their Christmas."

Maisy's sympathy was gone. "But leaving them when they need you the most is the answer?"

A flash of anger brought Sharleen's blood to a simmering boil. "What else am I supposed to do?"

"You're supposed to be there at 2:45 today with a smile on your face," Maisy said. "And do you know why it's important to smile at the kids you work with? Because it might be the only one a child sees today. You are hope to them, Sharleen. You understand them, where they come from, the struggles they face. From what I hear, the students are working very hard to bring this show together." Maisy took another sip of coffee before she continued. "You volunteered for a reason. Despite what you're telling me right now, you know how much you need to be there."

But my grandmother died. My parents are gone. I don't want this constant slap in the face every day seeing my old neighborhood.

Sharleen stared at Maisy. "Perhaps."

NINE

A Lot in Common

SHARLEEN COULDN'T BELIEVE her eyes. She was standing in the doorway of Alma's apartment, spare key still in the lock.

"What are you doing in my grandmother's apartment?" she demanded.

The older woman with puffy blonde hair seemed surprised by Sharleen's question. She gave her a haughty look and said, "We have a new tenant moving in. There's a crew here boxing up her belongings. Would you like for us to have them delivered to you?"

I'm about to murder this woman.

Stepping further into the apartment, Sharleen counted three men in matching T-shirts with the name of a local moving company printed on their backs. They were placing Alma's things in cardboard boxes. One of them stood by with a tape roller, ready to seal.

"I don't want anyone touching anything," Sharleen insisted. "How dare you come in here and do this. My grandmother hasn't even been buried yet."

The irritated woman placed a hand on her hip and let out an exasperated sigh. "I suppose you're here to do the work then? The new tenant moves in tomorrow morning. There's a waiting list, you know."

"I know. It took my grandmother almost two years to get in this place. I told her not to do it, but she wouldn't listen to me."

"And living with you wasn't an option?"

"No, it wasn't."

"Look," the woman said, "you can stand here and argue all day, but I need to get this place emptied out and cleaned by tomorrow morning, and the day is already half over."

"I just want some time to go through everything," Sharleen said. "She was the only living family member I had left."

"Almost everything is boxed up."

Sharleen's eyes moved to the curio cabinet in the corner of the room. "Not her cows," she noted. Although Sharleen had nowhere to put them in her own tiny apartment, she turned to the men in the room and said, "All of the cows are going with me. And, yes, I want them delivered."

Later that afternoon, Sharleen stepped off the bus and started on her two-block walk to the elementary school. She reached the middle of the first block and stopped. Curiosity made her cross the street.

Looking up, Sharleen stared at a drab split-level house. Sadness overwhelmed her. On impulse, she unlatched the front gate and entered the unkempt yard. She made her way to the creaky, wooden porch and sat on the top step. Within moments, Sharleen began to cry, remembering all the times she'd sat in that exact spot when she was younger. She closed her eyes and breathed deep, half expecting to catch the scent of her mother's legendary lasagna—her favorite dish to make on special occasions. She strained to hear, hoping her parents' words would drift out of the kitchen window and to her ears like they used to. Eavesdropping on them was a secret joy. Hearing them tell each other words of love and endearment used to bring a smile to Sharleen's face.

Opening her eyes, Sharleen longed to see her father at the gate, home from a long day at the garage. He'd walk across the yard, shoulders hunched over from exhaustion, empty lunch bag and thermos in hand. He'd stop at the bottom of the steps, look up at his daughter, and ask, "What new and exciting thing happened to you today?"

From her pocket, Sharleen pulled out the white velvet box. She opened it. Inside was a beautiful ring. Sharleen stared at it in awe and disbelief, recognizing the heirloom at once.

Lita's wedding ring. Her most treasured possession. What a beautiful thing to leave behind. And now, it's mine.

Sharleen stood and gathered her belongings. Seconds later, she left the yard, closing and latching the gate behind her.

She stepped off the curb to cross the street but tripped over her own feet in the process. She stumbled, stopping her fall by placing a palm against the side of a parked car. The box slipped from her grasp. Sharleen watched in horror as the it disappeared through the slats of a grate in the ground.

Immediately, Sharleen kneeled, trying to reach down, through the grate, to retrieve it. She could see it but it was out of reach.

What have I done? I can't lose this ring. Think, Sharleen, think.

She looked up, relieved by the sight of a familiar red pick-up truck.

Sharleen caught Jake's reaction when he spotted her sitting on the curb with her hand down the storm drain. He parked, got out of the truck and rushed toward her.

"I was just driving by and I saw you," he explained.

"Sorry," was all she could think of to say.

"What are you doing?" he asked. "Everything okay?"

Sharleen looked up, shielding her eyes from the late afternoon sun with her hand. "I need help," she admitted.

"Yes," he said with a chuckle and a nod, "it would appear that you do."

A rush of emotions surged forward. "My grandmother died yesterday, and she left me this ring. Only it's not just any ring, it was her wedding ring. It's been in my family for years. And it's the only thing I have left of her other than her porcelain cow collection."

"I see," said Jake. "And you dropped the ring down the drain?"

Sharleen lowered her eyes to the ground, feeling absurd and even a little ashamed. "Something like that."

She was shocked when Jake started to walk away, back to his truck.

On her feet, she shouted after him, "Where are you going? You're leaving?!"

He looked back and said over his shoulder, "Relax, I'm getting some tools out of my truck. Lucky for you I'm a contractor."

Ashamed of her outburst, Sharleen let out a small sigh of relief, and mumbled, "Yes … lucky for me."

Jake returned with his tools and started to work on fishing the ring box out of the drain. Sharleen stood close by, watching, waiting.

"I used to live here," she said. "In this house. A long time ago. When I was a kid. I actually went to the elementary school from Kindergarten through to the sixth grade."

Why am I telling him this? Let the man work. Stop talking, Sharleen.

"Sounds like there's a reason why you're back."

"I'm not sure what it is ... the reason," she said with a slight shrug.

"Well, for one, it was to bring a smile back to my daughter's face. Something I haven't been able to do myself."

"A smile," Sharleen repeated. "That reminds me of something I heard earlier today."

"To tell you the truth," Jake continued, "I haven't seen Ivy this excited about something in a few years. Not since her mother died."

"Your wife died?" Sharleen said, stunned.

I knew you weren't married, but I had no idea you were a widower.

"Yeah. I lost my wife to breast cancer. It's just been me and Ivy. Things have been pretty intense, and sad." He shifted his body and reach, trying a different angle and approach. "Until you showed up."

"Ivy is a very special girl," she said. "I'm sure I don't have to tell you that."

"Listen, I know we don't know each other very well, so this might be a strange thing for me to say ... but I have a feeling ... you're very special, too."

Jake's words hung in the air for a moment, mixing with the sunny November chill before floating into Sharleen's heart.

"My grandmother's gone now," she said. "And I lost both of my parents when I was seventeen. I woke up this morning and I realized I have no one. I'm not sure, but I think this is the worst feeling in the world."

"I'm very sorry to hear about your grandmother."

"Thank you."

Jake stood up and handed Sharleen the retrieved box. She clutched it tightly, scared to drop it again. She took a step back away from the storm drain, the curb, and Jake.

"You're welcome," he said. "I'm sure you're not in a festive mood, but Ivy and I have big plans to decorate our Christmas tree tonight—complete with the best homemade hot chocolate in the world. You're welcome to join us … if you want. No pressure."

Smiling for the first time that day, Sharleen responded with, "I'd like that."

Sharleen entered the school office with her entourage in tow: backpack and book bags. She approached the main counter.

Round two. Let's try this again.

Joyce looked up from her work, stood, and met Sharleen with a warm, welcoming smile.

"Joyce, I was wondering who I can talk to about ordering supplies for the holiday variety show?"

Joyce gave her a strange look as if Sharleen were speaking to her in another language. "Supplies?"

Sharleen reached into one of her book bags and retrieved a handwritten list. She handed it to Joyce.

"Yes. I've made a list of items we need," she explained. Joyce reached for her reading glasses on top of her head and brought them down to inspect the list. "As you can see, it's mostly stuff related to costumes. We do need some lumber and paint to build a set of some kind. And I would love to have the program professionally printed, if possible. And the stage lights are awful. I'm pretty sure they're a fire hazard waiting to happen."

Joyce offered Sharleen a look of compassion. "I can pass this list along to Betty," she said, "but I wouldn't expect much."

Optimism faded. Frustration kicked in. "I realize that the budget is limited—"

"Limited in the sense that there is none," Joyce said. "You want my advice? See what Willie can do to help with the paint and the lumber. She's very resourceful with these sorts of ... issues. The program can be copied on the machine here if it's fixed on time. I'll work on that. As for costumes, how well do you sew?"

"Unfortunately, home economics was the one class I flunked," said Sharleen.

Seconds later, she left the office.

Another strikeout. Defeated again. This place is in worse shape than I thought.

As she made her way to the multipurpose room, a group of students were gathered in a circle. At once, she knew a fight was happening. She pushed her way through the crowd for confirmation. In the center of the arena, a small Victor was defending himself against an older, bigger student. Sharleen recognized the other boy as Roger, Raquel's younger brother, who was just as big and apparently just as mean.

What is it with their family? Both of them are bullies.

By instinct, Sharleen intervened, physically separating the two boys. In the process, she was hit hard in the face. More surprised by the action than physically hurt, Sharleen staggered back a few steps before steadying.

"Both of you stop it!" she ordered. "Now!"

Holly suddenly emerged from her classroom. She marched to Roger and grabbed him by the collar of his hoodie.

"At it again, Roger? This is the third time this month!" Holly said.

"He started it," the freckled-faced boy insisted.

Victor wiped his mouth. Already, his bottom lip was swelling. "I did not! He called me names."

"Shut up, ballerina boy!" barked Roger.

Victor lunged at Roger, but Sharleen held him back with a strong arm.

Holly turned to Sharleen. "I can take it from here."

Sharleen froze for a few seconds as uncomfortable visions from her childhood flooded her mind. "Brings back a lot of memories, doesn't it?" she said to Holly. "Name-calling. Fighting. The bullying."

"Fighting is never a good thing," said Holly, "but it's important for Victor to know how to defend himself. Otherwise, he'll be picked on for the rest of his life."

Sharleen took a deep look in Holly's eyes. "Is that the lesson you were trying to teach me back then, Holly?"

Holly looked as if the question made her uncomfortable. "Look, we both know you won't be here long," she said. "So, we can just avoid each other until you leave. Deal?"

Sharleen slid an arm around Victor's shoulders. "I'd like to take Victor with me, if you don't mind."

"Suit yourself," Holly answered, followed by a dismissive wave of her hand. "It seems the two of you have a lot in common."

Willie looked concerned when Sharleen and Victor entered their room. She put down her cleaning rag and spray bottle of disinfectant cleaner and approached them.

"Who did that to his face?" Willie asked, inspecting Victor with a gentle hand under his chin.

"Stupid Roger," answered Victor.

"That boy is nothing but a bully," Willie said. "So is his sister. He's been picking on you all year."

"Willie, can you get some ice and meet us backstage?" Sharleen said. "I want to talk to Victor before the other students arrive for rehearsal."

Willie nodded and hurried off.

Sharleen and Victor walked up the steps and entered an area in the left wing. They walked through an open door into a dressing room. Sharleen turned on a light switch. Each dressing mirror flickered to life with the surrounding lights. She sat Victor down on a metal folding chair then kneeled beside him.

"You want to tell me what happened?" she asked.

Victor avoided her eyes. "No, not really." Thick strands of his dark hair hung in his eyes. He pushed them away.

Poor kid needs a haircut. And a hug.

"Maybe I can help, if you do," Sharleen offered.

"You can't help me, Miss Sharleen. No one can."

"Fighting won't solve anything," she said. "No matter how angry you get."

"I don't have a choice. My dad says I need to stand up to Roger." Tears filled his eyes.

"He also said I need to quit the show."

"Is that what you want to do?" Sharleen asked.

"No," he said. "I love dancing. But it bothers people when I do. I'm tired of them calling me names all the time."

"I know it isn't easy—"

"You have no idea," Victor snapped. "You don't live here like I do. You probably live in a fancy neighborhood where everybody has a dog and a clean house and nobody wants to hit you all the time."

Willie appeared in the doorway of the dressing room with a sandwich bag stuffed with ice. She handed it to Sharleen who placed it against Victor's cheek. He winced when the cold bag made contact with his skin.

"Thank you, Willie," Sharleen said with a smile.

Willie stepped forward. "Victor, you obviously don't know Miss Sharleen as well as I do."

"Oh, yeah?" he replied. "Is she your friend, too?"

"Yes, she's my friend. But she also grew up around here," said Willie. "In fact, she was a student here once—just like you."

Victor turned to Sharleen, brows scrunched. "You were?"

She smiled and nodded. "I was."

"And some of the kids used to tease her, too," Willie continued. "Because she loved to play the piano."

Victor let out a small laugh. "They made fun of you for that?"

"They did," Sharleen said. "And it used to make me mad."

"So, what did you do?" Victor asked.

"I kept playing. I didn't give up. Not even when things got tough for me," said Sharleen. "Not even when I lost my parents. I played until I got into college. And it lead me here … to you."

Victor looked like he was giving this some thought. "Wait," he said. "Don't you mean it led you *back* here? Back home? To us?"

"Yes," she said. "Exactly. The point is I didn't give up something that I love because other people wanted me to. I know it's not easy for you, Victor. Some people don't want boys to dance. They don't understand it. But you're not dancing for them."

After a moment's pause, he smiled. "I'm dancing for me?"

"Yes, and you're so good at it."

"You always say that, Miss Sharleen, and it's nice to hear, but…"

"Victor, do you know that you can study dance in college? And if you work hard at it, you can become a professional one day."

Willie spoke from where she stood in the near distance. "Miss Sharleen knows what she's saying, so I hope you listen to her. We're lucky she's here helping with the holiday show," she said. "Lord knows nobody else wanted to do it."

Sharleen turned to the older woman. "Speaking of which, do you think you can get your hands on some lumber and some paint for me?"

Willie gave her a look and said, "That depends."

"On what?"

"Cover your ears, Victor." He put down the bag of ice and complied with Willie's command. "Are you opposed to me breaking the law to make it happen?"

Sharleen cracked a grin. "No, not at all."

"Good," Willie said. "Then consider it done."

The rest of the afternoon seemed to fly by in a succession of moments that felt like the shuffling of cards.

Sitting at the piano, Sharleen led the students through vocal warmups. Ivy struggled with her confidence under the menacing eyes of Raquel and Camilla, but she powered through.

Later, on stage, Sharleen walked the students through the choreography of the finale. Again, Victor was clearly the best dancer in the group.

While most of the students rehearsed the opening number, Willie unloaded a portable cart filled with paint cans. She took them backstage with the help of Victor and Ivy, the first and only students to volunteer to help Willie with the task.

Sharleen grew nervous when she spotted a curious-looking Betty peering through a window in one of the double doors, watching the students rehearse.

It's okay. Don't stress. She looks happy with what she sees.

Minutes later, Sharleen sat down at the piano with a tape measure. She measured each student for costumes, writing their information down in a spiral notebook.

As the students left for the day, a few of them stopped to hug Sharleen, taking her by surprise.

Ivy and Victor asked for second hugs.

"You smell good, Miss Sharleen," Victor said.

"Thank you," she said, blushing.

"And you have a pretty smile," Ivy added. "Even my dad says so."

And he's got the cutest dimples I've ever seen.

TEN

Her Name was Penelope

As Sharleen left the building, she entered the almost-empty parking lot and joined Ivy who was waiting for her father to pick her up.

Ivy smiled the second she saw Sharleen, waving her mittened hands with enthusiasm. They stood together beneath the bare tree branches. The temperature was dropping. Sharleen shivered a little, despite all she was carrying and the thick jacket she wore. "You don't have to wait with me, Miss Sharleen," Ivy offered. "My dad should be here soon."

This is awkward.

"Actually, your dad invited me to spend some time with you guys this evening," Sharleen explained, with caution. "He said he mentioned it to you. I just want to make sure that's okay?"

Ivy's face lit up like the moon. Her eyes widened with excitement. "Of course it is!" she said. "Are you coming to our house?"

"Yes, I think so," Sharleen replied. Ivy's joy was infectious. Sharleen felt she was smiling from the inside out. "He said something about decorating a Christmas tree."

The expression on Ivy's face changed. Her excitement disappeared. For a brief moment, it seemed like she might cry. Then, she did.

"Ivy, I'm so sorry," Sharleen soothed. "I didn't mean to upset you."

"You didn't," Ivy insisted, sniffling. "My mom ... we used to decorate the Christmas tree together ... but since she died, my dad hasn't wanted a tree. I thought he hated Christmas. Maybe he doesn't hate it anymore because he met you." Ivy wiped her tears away with the back of her mitten. "I miss my mom a lot, Miss Sharleen."

"I know how you feel. I really do. I used to bake cookies with my mom every year for the holidays. Ever since she passed away, it's not the same."

Ivy looked up. She stopped crying. "Your mom died, too?"

Sharleen nodded, blinking back tears. "She did. And I miss her very much. Every day."

"Sometimes I get really sad when I think about her," Ivy shared. "But other times I laugh when I remember silly stuff she used to say and do."

"That's how people live on forever," said Sharleen. "When we talk about them, it keeps their spirit alive."

"Then maybe we should talk about our moms a lot. Maybe not every day, but a lot."

"Ivy, I want to be sure that you're okay with me spending time with you and your dad. If you just want me to be Miss Sharleen and only see me at school, that's okay."

Ivy reached out for Sharleen's hand and said, "But I like being with you. All of the time."

"I like being with you, too."

In the near distance, Sharleen spotted Jake's pick-up truck approaching.

"Quick," she said to Ivy. "Tell me. What's your favorite thing to eat for dinner?"

Ivy grinned. "Pizza, of course."

Jake arrived. He got out of the truck to help Sharleen with her backpack and book bags.

"Wow," he said, straining. "This stuff is even heavier than the last time. Do you collect rocks as a hobby?"

Sharleen laughed. "Just so you know, I asked Ivy if it was okay for me to hang out with you guys."

Ivy clapped her mittens together. "I said yes. C'mon. I'm hungry." She was already climbing into the truck, ready to go.

"You're always hungry," Jake said. He turned to Sharleen. "Any suggestions for dinner?"

"Pizza," Sharleen decided, with a wink in Ivy's direction. "It's the only option."

Jake looked amused. "Pizza, huh? I feel like this is a conspiracy."

Sharleen stepped closer to the truck. "Decorating a Christmas tree is hard work. Pizza will give us the strength we need."

The pizzeria was just as quaint inside as it was from the street. The entire restaurant was decorated for the holidays. Christmas music playing in the background added to the festive atmosphere.

Jake, Sharleen, and Ivy sat together in a booth. A lot of pizza had been consumed.

Sharleen pushed her plate away and announced, "I don't think I can eat another bite."

Ivy reached toward the middle of the table and helped herself to one of the two slices left. "I can."

"She's a bottomless pit when it comes to pizza," Jake said. "This is her favorite place to eat, but I think you already know that."

"I've actually never been here before," said Sharleen. "It's a very cute place."

Jake leaned in. Sharleen was tempted to reach out and push his shaggy dark hair out of his even darker eyes. He had the whole rugged and brooding thing down well. "Yeah, maybe we'll come back here again," he said, before adding, "Just the two of us."

"You mean ... like a date?" As soon as the words flew out of her mouth, Sharleen's cheeks flamed.

Could I be more presumptuous? Now he's going to feel obligated to say yes. When will I learn to think before speaking?

Yet, Jake didn't seem like he was dodging the question. In fact, when he answered it, Sharleen saw certainty in his eyes. "Yes, I think that's what they're called," he said, followed by a laugh. "It's been so long I honestly don't remember."

Ivy paused from eating long enough to add to the conversation at the table. "Daddy, don't be silly. Sharleen, say yes. Hurry, before he changes his mind."

"Yes," Sharleen said. "I would like that very much."

Ivy reached for her napkin, dabbed her face with it, and then asked, "Daddy, can we have ice cream now?"

Jake and Ivy entered their home with Sharleen following close behind. Once inside, she looked around, taking in the surroundings. The ranch-style single-story house was cluttered and felt chaotic, yet it exuded comfort and charm.

Sharleen started to take off her coat but paused when she spotted a family portrait on the wall near the front door.

"Your wife was a beautiful woman," she said.

Jake hung up his coat in a small closet. "Yes, she was. Her name was Penelope. Everyone called her Penny."

"Ivy looks so much like her."

"I know," he said, with a tender look in his eyes. He took Sharleen's coat from her and hung it up in the closet next to his.

Ivy appeared then. Already she'd managed to peel off her jacket, hat, mittens, and shoes. "Miss Sharleen, can we make hot chocolate together now? My dad usually makes it because he thinks his is the best in the world, but can we do it?"

"If that's okay with your dad, then sure we can."

Jake offered a nod of approval. "I'm outnumbered," he said. "I've never been able to say no to beautiful women."

In the large kitchen, Ivy and Sharleen made a pan of hot chocolate together, complete with marshmallows. While trying to help, Ivy accidentally sprayed Sharleen with canned whipped cream. Immediately, Sharleen could see regret on her face. To keep the mood light, Sharleen took the can and chased Ivy with it. They collided at the end of the hallway, laughing. Jake appeared with a stern look of disapproval, bringing the impromptu chase to an end.

Later, the three of them sat in front of the fireplace. Sharleen was on the comfy couch where she watched Ivy and Jake open a sealed cardboard box. Inside were Christmas ornaments that Jake explained had been in their family for years.

Sharleen took pause, feeling a sentimental avalanche of emotions she was struggling to hold at bay.

I miss my parents right now more than ever, our holidays together. They were so magical. Just like this.

"It's time to trim the tree," Jake said. "Sharleen, will you do the honor of placing the first ornament on the tree?"

Sharleen stood. "Of course. I'd be happy to."

Together, the three of them spent the next half hour trimming the once bare tree.

Finally, Jake plugged a string of lights into a socket, illuminating the branches with a variety of beautiful colors.

They stood back and admired their work.

"We did the tree justice," Jake decided. "Teamwork."

"She's asleep," Sharleen said as Jake drove her home later. Within seconds of the drive, Ivy nodded off, crashing against Sharleen and passing out. "Too much pizza, probably."

"One too many sugar rushes tonight," Jake said. "I'm going to have to cut her off from hot chocolate for the rest of the holiday season."

Sharleen smiled. "I think you'll have a fight on your hands if you do."

Jake stopped at a red light. He turned to Sharleen. His face was illuminated with the digital glow coming from the dashboard. "I had a really nice time with you tonight. I'm glad you decided to come over."

"I'm really glad you decided to invite me."

They stared at each other in silence, with a sleeping Ivy nestled between them.

This moment is everything. He looks so handsome. And the way he's staring at me—no man has ever looked at me that way before.

God, I hope he likes me.

The light turned green.

"I can't wait until we get to do this again," Jake said.

Beaming, Sharleen grinned from ear-to-ear and said, "Is tomorrow too soon?"

Half an hour later, Sharleen sat at her kitchen table with the intention of doing some late-night homework. Finals were right around the corner and she knew she needed to prepare for them.

Yet, it was difficult to concentrate. Sharleen replayed moments from the evening over again in her mind, cringing at some but smiling at most.

And then, she thought about her grandmother.

I wish you could be here, Lita, to see everything I'm doing and what's happening in my life. I wish Jake and Ivy could've met you. They would've loved you and you would've adored them, especially Ivy.

Saddened, Sharleen got up and went into her bedroom. Sitting on the edge of her unmade bed, she opened the drawer in her nightstand and took out the white ring box. She opened it and stared at the beautiful ring. Then, she glanced over at a framed photograph of her and Alma together. She picked up the picture and held it close to her.

She laid down on the bed, welcoming the soft texture of the pillowcase against her neck. Still holding Alma in her arms and the ring box in her hand, Sharleen started to cry. Within a few minutes, she drifted off to sleep, lullabied by the sweet, faint sounds of Christmas music playing somewhere in the not so far away distance.

It was as if Lita were hugging her back.

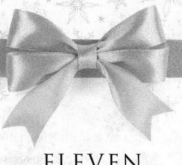

ELEVEN

You Need Help

WHEN CLASS ENDED, Sharleen started to collect her things. To her surprise, Professor Richter approached, a look of concern on her face.

"Forgive me if I'm being intrusive, but are you all right?" Lena Richter asked, once the other students were gone and out of earshot.

"I'm fine, Professor," Sharleen answered with a reassuring smile. "Why do you ask?"

"You haven't seemed yourself lately. I'm concerned. I'm just wondering if my hunch is right. I hope you know you can talk to me, Sharleen … about anything."

"Well … to be honest … my grandmother passed away last week." Sharleen stopped for a moment. Saying the words was still difficult, no matter how often she said them. It still hurt. "She was the only family member I had left, so adjusting to life without her hasn't been easy … but I'm trying to handle it as best as I can."

Professor Richter offered Sharleen an expression of deep sympathy and said, "I'm very sorry to hear that."

"Thank you."

"If you need anything…"

"And of course, the holidays are almost here," Sharleen continued, "and no one likes to spend Christmas alone."

"No, I can't imagine they would."

"Which is probably why I slept through Thanksgiving last week," said Sharleen. "On a brighter note, I got a new job. I'm working at my old elementary school in the neighborhood I grew up in."

"They must be happy to have you back."

"I just hope I don't let them down," Sharleen explained. "See, they've asked me to direct their holiday show. But this show is really important to the kids participating. And they're so talented … you should see them."

"For what it's worth, you don't seem like the type of person who doesn't rise to the occasion," Professor Richter said. "Or back down from a challenge."

"Thank you. I'm not exactly sure what you mean by that, but you're older than me and you're a professor, so clearly you know what you're talking about," said Sharleen, followed by a short nervous laugh.

"Let me put it into different terms," her teacher offered. "Sharleen, there's a reason you never learned to play the tambourine."

Sharleen replayed the conversation over again in her mind during the afternoon bus ride to her old neighborhood. While she was grateful for Professor Richter's concern, a plaguing thought would not leave her alone.

Am I destined to be a sad person for the rest of my life?

In Sharleen's twenty-four years, many of them seemed permanently scarred by one form of tragedy or another. The magnitude of each and the shadow they continued to cast over her world felt inescapable.

By the time she squeezed her way through the exit door of the bus and planted her feet back on familiar ground, Sharleen was convinced every person she met would somehow pity her.

Including Jake.

There was no doubt he had feelings for her, but she started wondering whether part of her appeal was the fact Jake wanted to take care of someone. He was the perfect prince in waiting, ready to rescue her at a moment's notice.

But I'm definitely no damsel in distress.

Or am I?

When she walked into the multipurpose room a few minutes later, she was surprised to see Maisy sitting at one of the tables. Dressed in her usual comfortable style, Maisy stood to greet her, holding a clipboard in her hand and a pencil tucked behind her ear.

"Hello," she said, sounding and looking stoic. "I'm here for your surprise onsite evaluation."

Sharleen placed her belongings on another table. Her backpack made a heavy thud when it met the hard surface. "What does that mean?" she asked.

"Well, you're a new employee," Maisy said. "All new employees are observed in their environment to make sure they're providing the best support possible for the students they're working with."

She's not making eye contact with me. I think she's lying. But why?

"I don't think that's true," Sharleen challenged.

Maisy tried to appear busy by writing on a piece of paper on her clipboard, but when Sharleen peered closer all she saw were scribbles. "Which part?" Maisy asked, still pretending to write something of significance.

"I think you're here because of Victor Salazar," Sharleen said. "Most likely because of his father, who I've been meaning to call, by the way. It sounds like he got to you first."

Maisy let out a sigh of exhaustion and looked up from her doodles. "Okay, I'm going to level with you," she said.

Sharleen grabbed a seat at the table. "That's better. Please do."

Maisy sat across from her. "Mr. Salazar did contact my office. I won't deny that," she said. "He had some choice words about his son participating in this show. The man sounds like an idiot, but who am I to judge? But he is the boy's father."

Sharleen's jaw tightened with anger. "You tell Mr. Salazar he can come down here and talk to me in person if he has a problem with me teaching his son to dance," she said, "and while you're at it, can you give the school board a call for me? Maybe ask them to help some very talented kids who need and deserve their support."

"Tell 'em yourself," Maisy shot back. "I'm not doing your dirty work for you. You want them to hear your demands, then go talk to them."

"I will," Sharleen assured her boss. Then, quickly added, "and how exactly do I make that happen?"

"There's a school board meeting next Thursday night. They have a microphone there for guests. Although I think you'll have no problem being heard." She met Sharleen's fiery stare from across the table. "Let me remind you that it is never our place to tell anyone how to raise their children. Even if we don't agree with a parent's choice, they're still the parent. We're not. Do we understand each other?"

"Yes," Sharleen replied, with a slight nod.

"Good. Now that we've got that out of the way, don't you have a show to rehearse?"

Sharleen got off the chair. "Yes, but Victor is still going to dance … but only if he wants to. That should be his choice." She left, anger still embedded in her veins, to meet the children flowing in.

Midway through rehearsal, Sharleen saw Maisy slip out the door, trying to do so without being detected.

I must have passed my fake onsite evaluation. Either that or Maisy has better things to do.

Still, Sharleen had to admit she was grateful to Maisy for her concern. She knew her boss only had her best interests in mind.

"You're all doing a wonderful job," Sharleen told the twenty-nine students who were on stage breathing hard, and sweating, and looking to her for approval. "But let's do it again. We only have a few more weeks to get it right."

Ivy raised her hand. "Miss Sharleen, where's Victor? He was in class but he isn't here."

That's an excellent question. I hope he's okay.

"I don't know," Sharleen answered.

"The dance isn't the same without him," Raquel offered. "He's better than all of us."

"Yeah," Camilla agreed. "Even though he's a boy, he's the best dancer in the show."

For some reason, hearing the belated praise for Victor triggered a strong response in Sharleen.

"Well, why don't you do Victor a favor and tell him that?" Sharleen suggested, hoping the anger simmering beneath the surface wasn't seeping through. "He'd probably like to hear that from someone other than me."

The students fell silent. They shifted uncomfortably, seeming awkward and unsure. They looked to Raquel for guidance since she was the biggest and oldest in the group.

"Miss Sharleen, are you mad at us?" Raquel asked.

"Yeah," added Camilla. "What did we do?"

Willie appeared then, poking her head through the doorway that led to the kitchen area in the far corner of the room. "Maybe they need a water break," she suggested. "Or maybe you do, Miss Sharleen."

Trying to walk off her emotions, Sharleen started to pace.

It's so damn dark in here. No wonder I'm sad. This place is like a cave—a sad, gloomy, pathetic cave.

"What we need in here is some sunshine." She was at the windows with both hands on the edges of the heavy drapes. With considerable force, she threw them open. Light shone in her eyes and covered her body, bathing her in the glow of December sunshine.

Look how much brighter it is in here. I should've done this on my first day.

Then, it happened. The curtain rods folded in on themselves and came tumbling down along with the drapes, crashing with a loud sound. Like weighted parachutes, the drapes did a swan dive to the floor.

On stage, the students all shared similar expressions of shock, wondering if their sweet director had really lost it this time.

"There," said Sharleen, making her way back to the piano. "That's better."

She sat down, cracked her knuckles, and placed her fingers above the keys, ready to play the opening number.

"From the top," she said.

Willie stepped further into the room. She joined Sharleen at the piano. "Well, look at it this way," she observed. "At least you have some fabric now. The color is pretty awful, but those drapes might make decent costumes."

Sharleen tried to keep a straight face, but it was no use. She laughed. Relieved by the joyous sound, the students laughed too, looking nervous but relieved.

"I tried to warn you,' Willie said, grinning. "This place will do it to you. I've seen stronger women than you lose their minds in half the time it took you."

I need to say something to the students to let them know I'm okay.

Sharleen stood and turned to address them. "Kids, the lesson of the day is … do whatever it takes to bring some sunshine into the world."

After rehearsal, Sharleen sat at one of the tables, exhausted.

Willie appeared and sat across from her. "You need help," she said, as a matter of fact.

"Don't remind me," said Sharleen. "Wait. What kind of help are you referring to?"

"The obvious kind," Willie said. "You need backup."

Sharleen was confused. "What … you mean like protection? I know how to defend myself, Willie. That's a rite of passage around here. Especially for girls who love to play the piano."

"You've got problems," Willie continued. "No budget. No money to buy cute costumes, or enough for fabric to sew a bunch of stuff— even with those nasty drapes you tore off the wall—nothing to decorate the stage with. You're gonna have these kids dancing barefoot on this rickety stage because you can't put dance shoes on their feet. These lights barely come on, and if they do, and you leave them on long enough, they'll probably burn the place down." Willie took a breath before continuing. "From where I stand, you only have one option."

Sharleen lowered her gaze. "Quit my job?"

"No," said Willie. "Something even better."

Intrigued, Sharleen leaned in. "Oh yeah?"

"Yeah," Willie said. "You need the mothers."

TWELVE
Hot Chocolate & Christmas Carols

SHARLEEN STOOD WITH Jake and Ivy at a gravesite. The grass beneath their feet was damp from an icy rainstorm that had just ended and was now heading south. Bundled up in hats, jackets, scarfs, and gloves, they huddled together staring at a specific headstone. The cemetery seemed still and calm, other than an owl that made his presence known with a delicate sound in the near distance.

"Are you sure you want me here?" Sharleen asked. "I can wait in the truck. Really, I don't mind."

Ivy looked up at Sharleen and said, "I wanted you to come here with us. So you could meet my mom."

Jake looked into Sharleen's eyes. "Ivy is convinced that you and Penny would've been friends."

"Best friends," Ivy insisted. "Miss Sharleen, do you think I'll ever see her again?"

"Yes. I do," said Sharleen.

"Do you think you'll see your mom again, too?"

"I do," she said. "I really do. But until then, I'm on my own. And that's okay."

Ivy looked at Sharleen with confusion on her young face. "No, you're not," she said. "You're not on your own."

Sharleen smiled. "I'm not?"

"No," Ivy explained, "because you have us now."

With that, Ivy slipped her hand into Sharleen's.

"Thank you, Ivy. That's very nice to hear."

"Are you coming over for Christmas?" Ivy asked. "I hope so. Maybe Dad will make us cinnamon pancakes."

"That's up to your father." Sharleen glanced up, waiting for a response.

Grinning at them, Jake replied, "As if I could say no."

The beautiful, twinkling gazebo was located in the center of a small, tree-lined park. It was the focal point of the town square. Sharleen, Jake, and Ivy sat inside it. Surrounded by awe-inspiring Christmas decorations, Sharleen felt like they were living inside the make-believe world of a snow globe. The magic was especially powerful at night. Even without the holiday festivities, the square possessed an irresistible quaintness that was picturesque and nostalgic.

She turned to Ivy who was busy sipping her cup of after-dinner hot chocolate and asked, "Is Christmas your favorite holiday?"

Smiling, Ivy answered with, "Miss Sharleen, I'm not sure who loves Christmas more—me or you."

Sharleen giggled. "I think we should have a sing off to find out."

Ready to accept the challenge, Ivy was on her feet. She carefully placed her cup of cocoa on the wooden bench. "Okay," she said. "Do we sing together?"

"We do," explained Sharleen. "Do you know the song, *Jingle Bells*?"

Ivy's face lit up. "It's one of my favorites."

"She sings it year-round," Jake said. "If it were up to her we'd have Christmas every day."

Ivy clapped her mittened hands in excitement when Sharleen said, "Let's sing it together."

Ivy froze for a moment. It was clear a thought of concern had entered her mind. "Should we sing quietly, so we don't bother people?" she asked.

"No," said Sharleen. "We're going to sing as loud as we want. Ready?"

"Yes!"

They sang the classic song together. Their voices blended in beautiful harmony. When the song was done, they laughed and embraced.

"Daddy, who's the winner?" Ivy asked, her arms still around Sharleen's neck. "Who loves Christmas more?"

Jake gave it some mock thought before replying. "I'd say it's a tie."

Ivy laughed. "You're just saying that because you love us."

"Yes," he said. "I do."

For Sharleen, it felt like time stopped.

Did I hear him right? Did he just say what I think he said? What is happening?

She stood. So did Jake. They met in the middle of the gazebo.

"Jake..." she said.

He reached out and took both of her hands into his. He looked deeply into her eyes. "Sharleen, I believe in speaking from the heart."

He's so nervous … and adorable.

She pulled him closer.

"Ivy," he said. "Cover your eyes."

Complying, Ivy covered her eyes with mittened hands but peeked through her fingers.

Jake and Sharleen kissed. It was a gentle, soft gesture.

Watching them, Ivy giggled.

"Merry Christmas, Miss Sharleen," Jake said.

She touched the side of his face with a gloved palm. "Merry Christmas, Jake Arlington."

Ivy joined them, trying to wrap her arms around their waists. She looked up at the adults and said, "If you two are going to stand here kissing in front of everyone, can I have another hot chocolate?"

Later that night, Sharleen sat on her sofa, lost deep in thought. Didn't even bother to undress from her night out with Jake and Ivy. The urge to pinch herself to make sure what she was feeling was real tempted her.

The night was perfect. It was like a fairy tale, a dream. I don't want this to end.

Finally, she stood, slipped off her jacket and scarf, then peeled off her gloves. Thirsty, she went into the kitchen but stopped half-way in. The sight of her lonely Christmas tree caught her eye. She moved to the table and leaned into the little tree. Picking up the photo of her parents, she stared at their faces. Her mother's eyes were filled with radiating joy. In one of the pictures, young Theresa was staring at young Guillermo with the same emotions that Jake made Sharleen feel.

Their love was so beautiful.

Sharleen closed her eyes and whispered, "Thank you for making me believe."

THIRTEEN

A Woman of Many Talents

$\mathcal{S}$HARLEEN KNOCKED ON the door of the professor's office before she entered. She gasped at the sight that greeted her.

Did I just walk into a gift-wrapping battle zone? Clearly, the paper is winning the war.

At her desk, Professor Richter was struggling to wrap a gift. In the process of doing so, it appeared the wrapping paper, ribbons, bows, and rolls of tape had turned against her.

"There are things in life I'm good at, Sharleen," Lena Richter explained. "Wrapping a Christmas present isn't one of them."

Sharleen laughed and moved closer. "Step aside," she said. "This is a job for a professional."

A look of astonishment came over the professor's face. "You're a professional gift wrapper? You really are a woman of many talents."

Sharleen went to work, fixing the damage her teacher had done. "I worked in a department store when I was sixteen," she explained.

"When they found out they could trust me with a pair of scissors and a roll of tape, I was gold."

"Lucky for me you're here," she said.

"Thanks."

There was a pause before Professor Richter spoke again. "Forgive me for asking this … but why are you here?"

Sharleen reached for the scissors. "I got a message you wanted to see me."

This stirred the teacher's memory. "Oh, yes. It's about your job."

Sharleen stopped moving. "My job?"

"Tutoring in the piano lab. The department received some unexpected grant money," said Lena. "You can start working again next semester. Isn't that great news?"

"Wow. Thank you."

"If I remember correctly, you said your job at the elementary school was temporary."

"Yes, it is," said Sharleen. "By the way, I hope you can make it to the show. The kids have worked very hard on it."

Lena gestured to her day planner sitting on her desk. "It's on my calendar. I wouldn't miss it."

Sharleen handed Professor Richter the wrapped present. "There." She smiled. "My work here is complete."

Lena beamed with gratitude. "I feel like I should pay you."

Sharleen shook her head. "You already have, Professor Richter."

Lena seemed touched by Sharleen's tone of reverence. "That's very kind of you to say." Then, a slender hand stopped Sharleen from leaving. "I almost forgot!"

Professor Richter opened a desk drawer and pulled out a gift bag of gumdrops. She handed the candy to Sharleen. "Here. These are for you. I know it isn't much, but I'm a teacher. You'll understand what I mean by that soon enough."

Sharleen smiled and laughed a little. "Thank you."

"My advice?" Professor Richter said. "Eat 'em while they're still fresh."

Sharleen nodded. "Yes, that's something I'll remember for the rest of my life."

FOURTEEN
The Mothers

As she pulled one of the squeaky double doors open and walked into the brightly lit multipurpose room, Sharleen expected the place to be empty as usual. Instead, three women blocked her path. They were standing shoulder to shoulder. One of them had her arms crossed. Another looked like she was a bodyguard. The smallest one teetered in her heels, as if she were either terrified or about to pass out. All three women looked a few years older than Sharleen.

"Am I being jumped?" At that moment, she realized the women were holding items in their hands. Her gaze shifted, taking in the considerable supplies they carried: measuring tapes, Christmas decorations, a handheld microphone. The female bodyguard was holding a steam iron and looked as though ready to knock someone out with it.

The one with the long hair and perfect black eyeliner moved in Sharleen's direction. "No, silly. I'm Sylvia. Sylvia Salazar."

"Hi, Sylvia. I'm Sharleen."

The menacing one offered her free hand to shake. "Name's Lola Gonzales."

"Hello, Lola." Sharleen shook her hand and immediately regretted it. "Ow."

The timid one with blonde hair and pixie bangs smiled and said, "Hello. I'm Cristina Morgenfeld."

"Hello," Sharleen said, still guarded. "Nice to meet you … all of you."

Sylvia lowered her voice to a whisper. "I heard you snapped and tore down those nasty curtains."

Sharleen nodded. "That was me."

"Good choice," Sylvia said. "It looks much better in here with some sunshine."

"Thank you." Sharleen continued to stare at them for a few minutes, mostly because they were staring at her. Finally, she asked the obvious question. "Why are you here?"

Sylvia gave Sharleen a look of confusion. "Willie said you needed us, so we're here."

Lola put down the iron in her hand and wrapped her arms around the other two, pulling them closer with such firmness that poor Cristina nearly came out of her shoes. Together, in perfect unison, they looked at Sharleen and announced, "We're the mothers!"

Later, on an extended water break, Sharleen worked with the students on a colorful wall display announcing the holiday variety show. They all gathered around the large bulletin board, each contributing helping hands and ideas. With diligence, Sharleen stapled the decorations to the surface, then stepped back to inspect their work.

"What does everyone think?"

A Kindergartener with a missing tooth said, "It looks pretty, Miss Sharleen, but it's all crooked."

"Oh, that's all right," she said. "Maybe if we leave it like this, people will think it has some charm."

Slinking around the corner of the hallway, Holly appeared in her usual attire of tight jeans and a cashmere sweater. Her dark hair was up in a slicked-back ponytail. Stuck to her side was her naïve sidekick, her permanent shadow. George was smiling, but Sharleen had no doubt that if she asked him why, he'd have to think before coming up with something along the lines of, "I've got nothing."

Holly stepped through the crowd of students to get a closer look at the bulletin board. "Hmmm," she said, her words hitting the wall. "Do you think people will even show up to something on a Saturday?"

George must've assumed Holly's question was directed at him because he answered it. "Yes." He stood, still grinning like a fool. "Yes, I do."

Holly snapped her head in his direction. He recoiled on the spot, as if he'd suddenly found himself in Medusa's line of evil vision.

Hanging his head in shame, George muttered, "No. No, I don't. It's a bad idea. Horrible."

Sharleen tightened her grip on the heavy stapler in her hand, tempted.

Killing her won't solve anything. And they'll definitely fire you for it. Then where will you be?

Forcing a smile, Sharleen said, "Holly. George. I hope you'll both be there to show your holiday spirit and to cheer the children on."

Holly's laughter sounded ridiculous and fake. "That depends," she said. "Will you be playing the piano?"

Put down the stapler, Sharleen. Walk away.

Sharleen held her wicked stare. "As a matter of fact, I am."

Holly stepped forward, just barely missing the tip of Sharleen's shoe in the process. "Then I'll be there," she said, with both hands on her hips. "In fact, I wouldn't miss it for the world ... your encore performance."

Holly turned on her heel and sashayed down the hallway, as though parading on the runway at a couture fashion show. George stayed behind. He continued to stare at the wall display, seemingly pleased with what he saw.

"This is a really nice display," he said to the students. He turned to Sharleen and added, "They're very lucky to have you."

From the other end of the hallway, a loud voice bellowed, "George!"

He jumped to attention and scurried off, like a frightened mouse being pursued by an invisible cat.

Raquel stepped in Sharleen's direction. She twisted a finger around one of her Shirley Temple curls and said with slight trepidation, "Miss Sharleen, can I ask you a question?"

"Sure, Raquel. You can ask me anything."

The tall, broad-shouldered girl dropped her gaze to the ground and asked, "Do I act like Miss Holly?"

"What do you mean?"

"Like the way I make fun of Ivy about being scared to sing? And how I always tell Camilla what to do."

Camilla looked up from the plastic tub of holiday decorations she was sorting through, even though the decorating was already done. "She's bossy," she said to Sharleen. There was a new boldness in her eyes when she looked at Raquel. "You're bossy."

Sharleen reached out and urged them to come closer. They did. She kept her words quiet as Ivy was nearby. "Why do you think you give Ivy a hard time about singing in front of people?"

Raquel shrugged. "I don't know. Maybe it's because I wish my voice was as good as hers."

"But it's not." Camilla's blunt response made Sharleen smile.

Apparently, Camilla woke up this morning and decided she wasn't taking any more of Raquel's orders.

In response, Raquel shot Camilla a look of death.

"What?" Camilla said, not backing down. "It's true. Just ask Miss Sharleen if you don't believe me."

Sharleen turned at the sound of approaching heels. Betty was dressed to impress, as usual, in a cream-colored power suit and a string of pearls. She smiled at everyone.

"Well, would you look at this?" she said, marveling at the display. "We have some very talented artists among us."

"Do you like it, Mrs. Marchant?" Ivy asked.

"I do," the principal said. "I think it looks wonderful."

"Miss Sharleen let us pick out the decorations," Camilla explained. "She always wants to hear our ideas."

"That's because she knows the best ideas come from others," Betty said. She turned to Sharleen. "I hear the cavalry has arrived in the form of, the mothers."

"Yes. They've been a huge help, but we could still use more. Better lights. A piano that's been properly tuned. A budget. Dance shoes. Some Christmas magic. A miracle or two."

Sharleen flung a hopeful stare at the principal.

The expression on Betty's face shifted to one of reverence. "I really admire what you've been able to do with nothing, Sharleen. It's very impressive. And I'm not the only one who's noticing. Willie raves about you … as do the parents. Your love for this school … well, it's apparent to all of us."

For a brief moment, Sharleen thought about her grandmother and how much she wished she were standing in the hallway with her, to hear firsthand all that Betty was saying. She blinked back tears as emotions swelled with intensity. "This school means a lot to me," she said. "It always has. Being back here … it's been good for me, Betty." Sharleen stopped. "Oops. May I call you Betty?"

"Of course, but only when students are not present. Otherwise, I'm Mrs. Marchant to everyone. It's important that we lead by example and show respect for those who have earned it."

"Yes, Mrs. Marchant," Sharleen said, suddenly feeling like she was back in the sixth grade."

Betty leaned in. "I know you want the show to be the best it can be. As do I."

"I do, which is why I'm going to the school board meeting tomorrow night," Sharleen whispered in reply. "I only need a few minutes to speak, to convince them to give you more money."

"And I hope that works."

"It will."

"But if it doesn't … the show will still be wonderful."

Sharleen took a step back. "You sound like you've given up hope. Have you?"

"No, just trying to be realistic. I've been asking for a bigger budget since I walked in the doors five years ago. It hasn't happened yet."

Sharleen straightened her posture. Over Betty's shoulder, she saw their faces: the students who needed her and were depending on her. She would fight with everything she had to get them more. There was unwavering confidence in Sharleen when she spoke. "Well, now you have me."

On her way to the bus stop, Sharleen saw Victor through the chain-link fence. She stopped in her tracks and stared. He was alone, sitting in one of the old swings. From his slumped posture, he looked defeated.

Without a second thought, she marched inside the school, rushed to the first exit she could find, and made her way to Victor's swaying seat on the fenced-in playground. As she moved, a wintry wind le her face stinging from the cold. Yet the temperature wasn't going to deter her.

Victor looked up as she approached. He wore a jacket that looked too big for him and a beanie cap that did its best to cover his overgrown dark hair. She couldn't tell if he was happy to see her or annoyed—or a bit of both. "Miss Sharleen, what are you doing out here?"

He looks so lonely. I'm not sure what to do or say.

Sharleen swallowed her doubts and said the first thing that came to her mind. "I saw you sitting here and thought you might need a friend."

His dark brown eyes were cast to the ground. "Aren't you supposed to be inside rehearsing for the show?"

"Rehearsal is over for the day. Besides, this is more important." Victor looked up. She held his gaze for a moment. His eyes reflected immense sadness, an emotion she was all too familiar with. She gestured to the empty swing next to Victor and asked, "Mind if I sit?"

He gave a slight shrug. "Suit yourself. It's a free world." Sharleen dropped her book bags on the asphalt and then struggled to get her backpack off. Watching her, Victor asked, "Why do you always carry so much stuff with you?"

"Well, I leave my house early in the morning and I don't get home until late at night. These are all the things I need for the day," she explained, fully aware that what she was telling Victor was only a half-truth.

"I always see you walking and everything looks so heavy," he noted.

"It is. Maybe someday I won't have to carry so much around with me."

"I bet you're going to try to convince me to come back to the show."

"No, I'm not," she said.

"You're not?"

"You know you're always welcome to come back to rehearsal, Victor. But that choice should be yours," she explained. "We miss you a lot, though. Even Raquel and Camilla told me how much they wish you were still dancing."

"They do?"

"Yes. Actually, everyone agrees you're the best dancer in the show."

"You always say that, too."

"Because it's true."

Victor moved a little in his swing, rocking back and forth gently. Sharleen noticed both of his shoes were untied. "Roger got suspended for three days," he said.

"Yes, I heard."

"When he comes back to school, he's probably going to hit me again because he'll be mad."

"If he does, I want you to tell someone."

"What for?" he asked.

"Because Roger was told if he hit you again, he'd be expelled."

"What difference will that make? He lives across the street from my house."

Sharleen took a deep breath, emotions swirling inside of her like a slow-building cyclone. Victor had her heart and she knew it. "I'm sorry you're going through this."

"It's okay," he said. "It's not that bad, I guess. My mom loves that I dance, but my dad … he told me I need to man up. I'm not even sure what that means." He stopped swinging. "Did anyone ever hit you … for playing the piano?"

Sharleen lifted her gaze to the school in the near distance. It seemed so much smaller than she remembered. "Yes, a very mean girl hit me … but it only happened a few times."

"Did she move away and go to another school?"

"No … I hit her back and knocked two of her teeth out," Sharleen said. "After that, she never hit me again."

"So, you think I should knock Roger's teeth out?" He sounded enthusiastic about the idea.

"As tempting as that probably is, no … I don't think you should do that."

"But if I don't do something, people will always call me names."

"You're right. They might," she said. "I don't want to lie to you and say it will stop, in case it doesn't."

"I want it to stop … more than anything."

"What else do you want more than anything?" she asked.

"I want to be in the show. I want to dance, Miss Sharleen." There was a new energy in his words, passion. "I feel happy when I'm dancing."

"That's all I want for you, Victor." She smiled down at him. "To be happy."

"What about you? Do you think you'll be happy soon?"

Sharleen felt as if her soul had been touched. That young Victor was turning out to be one of the smartest, most intuitive persons she knew—and he was only ten. It was a struggle not to cry.

No one has ever asked me that question before.

Jake and Ivy flashed in her mind. The night in the gazebo. Decorating the Christmas tree together. The cemetery. "Yes, I do," she said, for once believing this to be true.

"Really?" Victor sounded surprised. "Why?"

Sharleen breathed in the icy air letting it invigorate her. "Because I'm tired of being sad."

Victor nodded, his back straightening from the stooped position. "Yeah … me too." He stepped out of the swing and stood in front of Sharleen. He stuck out his pinky and asked, "Can we make a promise?"

"What kind of promise?" she asked.

"That if we start to feel sad a lot, that we tell each other," he said. "Then I can dance and you can play the piano and we'll both be happy again."

"That sounds perfect." She hooked her pinky around his and said, "I promise."

"Good." He cocked his head, a serious look crossing his features. "Miss Sharleen, I have one other question."

"What is it?"

To her surprise, Victor reached for her backpack and picked it up off the ground, straining to do so.

He wants to help me put my backpack on … the way I help him.

The haunting expression in Victor's deep brown eyes was a mixture of gratitude and hope. His shoulders lifted and fell as he inhaled a deep breath, then exhaled. "Is it okay if I come back to rehearsal tomorrow?"

FIFTEEN

Ashes

SHARLEEN AND IVY were sitting on the living room floor working on costumes for the show. Nearby, the decorated Christmas tree twinkled and blinked as though saying hello. A fire crackled in the fireplace. From the kitchen, delicious aromas floated in the air.

Jake was busy cooking an elaborate dinner. Earlier in the day, he'd texted Sharleen and invited her over for a home-cooked meal, a mini feast for the evening including his specialty, beef stroganoff, along with steamed asparagus, garlic mashed potatoes, and a bottle of wine for the adults, and apple juice for Ivy.

The invitation had been too irresistible to turn down.

It had been a few days since they were able to spend time together. Jake explained he'd been busy with a new project as a contractor. Sharleen was dealing with an equally full schedule: preparing her students for the show, studying for final exams, and trying to decide what she was going to do with the three boxes of porcelain cows now gracing the middle of her apartment.

When Jake appeared in the entryway of the living room looking somewhat flustered, Sharleen lifted her eyes from a complicated stitch. "Everything smells so good. I picked the right house to have dinner at tonight."

"My dad is a very good cook," Ivy boasted.

Jake grinned. "Dinner will be served shortly, my ladies." He turned to his daughter. "Ivy, can you set the table?"

Ivy jumped up and started working on the assigned task. In the process, she picked up Sharleen's heavy backpack, dropping it. The bag hit the hardwood floor in the dining room with a hefty bang. Out of the backpack rolled an object, spinning across the floor in what looked like slow motion when it collided with the edge of Jake's shoe, stopping. He stared at it, and a flash of realization covered his curious face.

Sharleen felt her cheeks singe with embarrassment. It was a moment of truth she wasn't prepared for.

Ivy was intrigued, but also looked fearful. "What is that?" she asked.

Jake looked at her and said in a calm voice, "Ivy, can you go to your room for a few minutes? I'll call you when we're ready to eat."

Ivy complied and left the room, disappearing down the hallway and into her bedroom. She closed the door. A few seconds later, the faint sounds of *Jingle Bells* could be heard in the near distance.

Sharleen stood, reached down and picked up the urn. She shoved it into her backpack, next to its identical deep burgundy and gold twin.

Jake looked at Sharleen for an explanation, but she remained silent, avoiding his gaze. Finally, his words cut through the stillness and silence, bringing the moment of aftermath to a necessary end. "You carry those around with you everywhere you go?"

Sharleen nodded, a strained and uneasy movement at that moment. "Yes."

"Are they your parents' ashes?"

"Yes," she said. "They were both cremated ... not by choice. Their bodies were so damaged in the fire there was almost nothing left of them. I'm not really sure how much of these are actually their ashes. They gave these to me to make me feel better, I think."

"And do you?"

"No," she said with honesty. "Jake, seven years have gone by and the pain hasn't gotten any easier. Having them with me wherever I go ... I know it doesn't make sense ... but it makes life more bearable."

She shut her eyes for a moment but opened them when he placed gentle hands on her shoulders.

"I understand how difficult it is to let go."

She looked up into his dark eyes. "I know you do."

"I used to go to the cemetery every day," he explained. "The first year. Like clockwork. I was up at the crack of dawn every morning. I even had the sprinkler schedule at the cemetery memorized by heart. The grounds crew knew me there by name. It was very important for me to show up each morning and talk to Penny. For her to know I was there. I felt like I had something to prove." He stopped for a moment and Sharleen wondered if he was struggling not to cry. "But as time went by and life went on, I stopped going as much. Now we go a couple of times a year. But it doesn't mean I love or miss Penny any less. And it doesn't mean the pain isn't still there."

"I want it to get easier," she said. "I really do."

"There's no time limit on sadness, Sharleen. There's no magical day or number in which everything suddenly feels normal again."

"I think why it's hard for me to let go is because they were all I had," she said. "That night is something I can never forget. It feels like it all happened yesterday. It was a Thursday night and I was out with my friend Ruby. I was seventeen. We were both graduating from high school in a couple of weeks, so we decided to stay out late and break our curfews, knowing there would be hell to pay. I remember thinking to myself that I'd made it through high school without getting into trouble once, unlike Ruby who was permanently grounded for something she did or didn't do.

When Ruby and I pulled up to my house, I saw the fire trucks and the crowd and the flames and I knew … I knew in that second my parents were gone and that nothing would ever be the same again." Sharleen stopped and took a breath, fighting the urge to fall apart in Jake's dining room. "And I was right. Because of faulty wiring in an old house and a dead battery in a smoke alarm, I became an orphan instantly. It doesn't seem fair."

"Because it's not," Jake offered. "I can't even imagine what you've gone through since then."

Sharleen reached for his hands and held them. "And now my grandmother is gone, too. I went to her funeral last week and five people showed up, Jake. That's it. A life spanning more than seventy years and only five people were there to show their respects. It broke my heart. She deserved so much more."

"I'm so sorry. I would've gone," he said. "I would've gone with you."

"It's my fault because I didn't ask."

He gave her a look. "And why didn't you? Ask, I mean."

"Because I've never felt so alone," she explained. "This grief is mine. It's not fair for me to make you suffer through it, too."

"But you're not alone, Sharleen."

"That's very sweet of you to say…"

"It's the truth." His tone had become firmer. "Ever since we met, we've both been doing the same thing."

"And what's that?" she asked.

"Resisting," he answered. "You and I are both sad people. We've experienced a greater sense of sorrow than a lot of people we know. But we can't let that grief stand in the way of happiness … we can't be defined by what we've lost. If we do, you and me … we'll never get the chance we deserve."

"I want that," she said. "I want that more than anything. For the grief to lessen … and for you and me to just go for it and give it a shot … no matter how crazy that might sound."

He walked her to the dining table and gestured to an empty chair. She sat. He kneeled, took her hand in his, and stared deeply into her eyes. "Listen, I know it's not the same thing … but me and Ivy … we'd love to be your family now."

Sharleen sniffled. "I don't want to cry in front of you."

Jake cracked a grin. "Would it help if I go first?"

She gave him a strange look. "You want to cry together?"

"Yes," he said, giving her hand a gentle squeeze. "I want us to do everything together." He kissed her cheek, lips gentle and warm on her skin. "Including letting go."

"I'm scared to, Jake," she admitted. "I don't want to forget them. Ever."

"I believe I know you well enough to say … you won't let that happen. But just because people we love are gone … that doesn't mean we should stop living."

She touched the side of his face with the back of her hand. "I'm sorry about the urns. I know it's weird and creepy and strange."

He let out a nervous laugh. "Yeah, just a little." Jake stood. "But I get it."

Sharleen looked up at him. "Thank you."

"Don't thank me yet. Wait until you taste my cooking. Then you'll really be thankful."

"I'm starving."

Right on cue, her stomach rumbled. They laughed.

"I'll go tell Ivy the coast is clear," he said. "Then the three of us can share our first family dinner together."

Sharleen nodded. "That sounds perfect."

SIXTEEN

Be My Backup

THE MULTIPURPOSE ROOM was buzzing with activity. There was an electric hum in the air, due in part to the three sewing machines in action.

Between two tables, Sharleen, Willie, Lola, Cristina, Sylvia, and Ivy, were hard at work. They were cutting fabric, sewing, ironing, painting pieces of the set, and even cleaning. Each had a look of intense focus on their faces, diligently working together as a dedicated team.

"It looks like Santa's workshop in here," Ivy said, words tripping out with pure excitement.

"Don't you mean Sharleen's workshop?" Cristina joked.

"Sharleen, I wish you were Santa," Lola said. "I have a long list for you of things I need, starting with a vacation."

"You're not lying," added Sylvia. "I've always wanted to go on a cruise and eat lobster all day."

"Yeah," Lola agreed. "That sounds real nice. When are we going, Sylvia?"

Sylvia laughed. "Probably the twelfth of never."

Needing to stretch her legs, Sharleen stood and walked the perimeter of the room. Since the drapes had yet to be replaced, the outside world could be seen with vividness. Night had fallen. The December sky seemed to sparkle with a heavy blanket of stars. The parking lot adjacent to the school was almost empty. Across the street, porch lights were on. She could see someone's television screen through their front window, although she couldn't determine what they were watching.

Sharleen turned and looked at her hard-working troop. Immense gratitude washed over her.

I need to let these people go home and be with their families. Or at least feed them. I should buy everyone pizza. I know Ivy wouldn't argue with that.

Then, Sharleen remembered what day it was. Thursday. The night of the board meeting. Throughout the day she'd wrestled with the same dilemma, *should I go and ask for support? Do I have it in me to do this?*

While glancing out the window, Sharleen became aware that Sylvia was standing next to her. She looked nervous, as if she were gathering up the courage to say something. "I'm not really good with saying soft stuff like Cristina is," she started, "but I just wanted to tell you I appreciate what you've done for my son."

Then, it dawned on Sharleen. She knew the trio collectively as the mothers—but who were they the mothers of?

I've been so self-obsessed, I never took a moment to ask them who their children were. I've been working alongside these wonderful women for three days and not once have I asked them any-

thing about their lives. Did they mention any of their children by name? And if so, did I completely miss it? What is wrong with me?

"Your son?" she asked, knowing very well she should've known the answer to her question.

Confusion covered Sylvia's face. "I'm Victor's mom," she explained. "I thought you knew."

"Of course, you are," Sharleen replied. She knew she could trust Sylvia, who wouldn't judge her, so she asked the question. "And Lola and Cristina? Who are their kids? I know, I know. I should've asked this sooner."

"It's no big deal. You've been so busy, I don't even know how you've had time to even think. Raquel and Roger belong to Lola. She got stuck with those two heathens. She swears she was cursed. And Cristina is Camilla's mom. Of course, Victor is mine. He's my only child. And Ivy belongs to Jake. All of the moms are secretly crushing on him, by the way. But we can tell he only has eyes for you."

"He's an awesome guy." Sharleen moved closer to Sylvia. "It sounds like your husband isn't too keen on the idea of having a son who's a dancer. It's not my business, and I'm not trying to interfere, but I'm worried about Victor. He really wants to dance in the show."

A gentle sigh escaped from Sylvia, even though her shoulders tensed up. "I think my husband will come around eventually," she said, not sounding very convincing.

"For Victor's sake, I hope so."

"My son is very special," Sylvia said. "He isn't like the other kids, especially the other boys. He never has been. But it's difficult for my husband."

"Imagine how difficult it is for Victor," Sharleen offered.

Sylvia leaned in closer. Sharleen saw the deep love the woman had for her son. It was in her eyes. "What am I supposed to do?" she asked. There was a hint of desperation in her words.

"Maybe just try letting Victor be who he is and loving him for it," Sharleen suggested. "You're his mom, so you know what's best for him. I just know how talented he is, Sylvia. He has a lot of potential."

"You really think so?" Sylvia furrowed her manicured brows together, waiting for the response.

Sharleen nodded. "The most important thing is he's found something he loves to do."

"Yeah," Sylvia agreed. "His little face lights up every time he talks about it."

"Maybe a first step could be getting him signed up for an actual dance class."

"He would love that." Sylvia paused for a moment as if she were contemplating an idea. "Do you think you could help me with that, Sharleen? Getting him signed up for something like that, I mean. Maybe we could find a class for him together."

"Sure," Sharleen said with a smile. "I'd be happy to help. In the meantime, can you ask him to come back to rehearsal? We all miss him."

Sylvia nodded. "Consider it done."

Lola approached them, but Sharleen couldn't read her expression. "Did you ask her yet?" Her words were directed at Sylvia.

Sylvia scowled at her. "Damn, girl. Gimme a second. We had some other stuff to talk about first."

"Ask me what?" prompted Sharleen.

Lola and Sylvia exchanged a look before Sylvia said, "Okay ... see ... back in the day me and Lola and Cristina used to be in a singing group. That's how we met." Sylvia fidgeted, raked fingers through her long dark hair, cracked her knuckles, picked at pieces of invisible fuzz on her sweatshirt. "Nothing ever came of it, but … we were thinking … could we sing in the show? It would be like a reunion for us … on stage."

Cristina joined them then. "It would mean so much to us," she added.

"And to our husbands," Lola said. "They've never seen us perform before because we were so young back then. It was a long time ago."

Sharleen gave the idea some thought before turning to the mothers. "I'll make the three of you a deal."

They leaned in, anxious.

"Speak your terms, girl," Lola said. "We're listening."

"I'm going to a school board meeting tonight," Sharleen said, deciding this on the spot. She glanced at the clock on the wall and realized she needed to leave in fifteen minutes, otherwise, she'd never make it to the meeting on time, especially by bus.

So much for dinner. And now I really want pizza, too.

"A school board meeting?" Lola repeated. "For what?"

"Because I need them to give this school a bigger budget," she explained.

"Why?" Sylvia asked. "Are we broke?"

"You don't know?" Sharleen said. "The board gives this school the smallest budget out of all of the schools in the entire district."

Cristina looked crushed by the information. "But why?"

From where she sat at a sewing machine, Willie spoke out. "Why do you think?" she said. "It's because of where we live. It's because of our zip code."

"Yeah," agreed Lola. "It's because this isn't 90210."

"Not even close," Sylvia said.

Still sewing, Willie explained to the mothers, "Sharleen has been fighting to get more money for the show and the school since she got here. She refuses to take no for an answer."

Lola looked at Sharleen for confirmation. "For real?"

Sylvia seemed equally impressed. "This school means that much to you, Sharleen?"

"Yes, it does. Mostly because I used to be a student here years ago. This is the neighborhood I grew up in … but I've been away for seven years. Way too long."

Sylvia was beaming with excitement and pride. "Yeah, I thought you were one of us," she said. "I had a feeling about you. Since you're younger than us, it's probably why I don't remember you from back then. Do you have any brothers?"

"No. I'm an only child … just like Victor."

Sylvia gave this some thought. "What about sisters?" she asked. "Because if you don't, you do now."

"Sylvia's right," Cristina said. "Already you feel like family to us."

"Yeah, we're your ride or dies now, girl. So, what do you need?" Lola asked. "What can we do to help?"

"I need you to go with me tonight," Sharleen said. "I need you to be my backup."

"Say no more," Lola insisted. "We're there."

"Thank you," said Sharleen. "And even though the show is supposed to be about the kids, I'll think about having the three of you perform in it. But only one song, so we can keep the focus on the students. Does that sound fair?"

The mothers looked at each other, mulling over the countered proposal. They nodded to each other. Sylvia looked at Sharleen. "Yeah, we can work with that."

"I know we still have a lot of work to do here, but we need to leave now if we're going to be on time for the meeting," Sharleen explained.

"I'll go as long as Cristina doesn't drive," Sylvia said. "And as long as my son can be there to watch you in action, Sharleen. We can pick him up on the way. Let me text him so he's ready."

"I think that's an excellent idea," Willie offered. "You should take Ivy, too. Let them watch someone stand up for something they care about."

"What about you, Willie?" Sharleen asked. "Will you join us?"

"Couldn't keep me away. I was just waiting to be asked."

Ivy stepped forward and asked, "Miss Sharleen, can you text my dad and ask him if I can go?"

How could she refuse those wide, pleading eyes? Sharleen pulled her phone out of her pocket and said, "I'm on it."

"Can we get some food on the way?" Lola asked.

"Yes, please," Sharleen agreed. "And it's my treat."

"You don't have to do that," Sylvia said. "We should be buying you dinner."

"It's the least I can do, considering how hard all of you have worked to make this show happen. Seriously, I wouldn't be able to do this without you."

Lola put an arm around Sharleen's shoulders. "Hey, that's what friends are for."

Friends. Did she just say we're friends? How did this happen? I can't believe these women have welcomed me into their lives.

As they packed up their things and headed toward the double doors, Cristina stopped and stared at Sylvia. "Hey," she said. "What's the matter with the way I drive?"

Sylvia laughed. "No offense, Cristina, but you drive like a nun."

SEVENTEEN

Public Comment

WHEN THEY ARRIVED at the local community center, Sharleen was surprised by how many cars were parked in the adjacent lot. Grateful for their support, she watched with pride as each one piled out of Lola's minivan. Together, the group walked to the entrance of the chic-looking modern building, complete with a slanted roof. The bright glow from within the building mesmerized her. The center looked like an illuminated beacon of hope, promising only good things to those who entered it. She took this as a good sign.

Inside, the lobby was buzzing with conversation and activity. Looking around at the sea of faces, Sharleen struggled with the sudden feeling she was out of place.

This is crazy. Why am I here?

Trying to quiet her inner critic, she approached a check-in table which was being manned by none other than Holly, who was dressed festively for the occasion, resembling one of Santa's sinful elves. Not a hair or false eyelash out of place.

Well, would you look who's here? They'll probably name her the Volunteer of the Year and give her an award or a parade. The mayor might even give her a key to Harmonville or create a holiday in her honor.

Holly raised a perfectly arched eyebrow at her. "Yes?" she greeted with her usual sneer.

"Hello, Holly," Sharleen said, keeping her volume up to be heard above the surrounding crowd. "I understand there's an opportunity to speak to the school board members tonight."

Holly skimmed a printed document in her hand before asking, "Did you sign up for Public Comment?"

Wonder if her brow is permanently arched like that?

"No. What is that?"

A look of sheer annoyance swept across Holly's face. "You have to sign up ahead of time for the Public Comment portion of the agenda, Sharleen. Did you do this?"

That condescending tone beat a banshee's wail, irking Sharleen. "No, I didn't," she admitted. "I didn't know that was a requirement."

"Well, then, you won't be able to speak tonight. The board will meet again in late January. The information is available on the website." Holly looked beyond Sharleen and said, "Next!"

"But I can't wait until next month. We need their help now. You know this. You work there."

"I'm sorry. There are no exceptions to the rule." Holly's words were firm. "You're welcome to attend the meeting tonight, but you won't be permitted to speak."

Sensing there was an issue, Sharleen's backup joined her at the check-in table, standing behind her like an army, flanking her on all sides.

"Is there a problem here?" Sylvia asked, her eyes locked on Holly.

"She says I have to sign up ahead of time to speak," Sharleen explained. "Honestly, I didn't know."

Sylvia continued to eye their nemesis. "Oh, you're gonna speak tonight, Sharleen."

"How?" she asked.

Lola stood next to Sharleen. "Leave it to me," she said. "I'll take care of it."

"Maybe we should go inside and find seats," said Cristina. "It looks crowded."

Willie laughed as they walked away. "And miss all the fun out here? This is the best night out I've had in years. I was kinda hoping Sharleen would finally come to blows with Holly. For old time's sake."

"That's not happening," Sharleen assured her.

Willie didn't bother hiding her disappointment.

Sharleen led the way, taking them inside the large, brightly lit room. Above them, expensive-looking light fixtures resembling UFOs cast a warm, comforting glow over the entire area. The seats themselves were cushioned folding chairs, an upgraded version of the chairs backstage at the school. They were crammed together as closely as possible. On the opposite side of the room stood a large, elevated platform. From left to right there were six board members seated at a long table covered with an elegant cloth. Sharleen noticed that the chair reserved for Jessica Spencer, the superintendent, was empty.

I really need her to be here tonight. Please don't let her be a no-show.

As they searched for seats, Sharleen took a moment to study each member seated onstage. Four men. Two women. Only one of them a person of color. All of them looked to be at least fifty years old, if not closer to seventy. They all shared a similar expression that suggested they'd rather be anywhere else than sitting at a table waiting for a public school board meeting to start. There was a folded name card in front of each member: Robert, Iris, John, Clark, Dottie, and Peter.

Sharleen tried to determine whether or not any of the board members would be sympathetic to her cause. Would they listen to her and understand why their support was so critical?

Please let me use the right words. Let me connect with these strangers who have the power to change everything for the school, for the kids.

Sylvia found empty seats for them in the fifth row from the front of the stage. They side-stepped their way through the very narrow aisle of chairs and sat, shoulders and knees touching.

"I didn't realize this many people cared about education," Willie observed. "Imagine if they all donated a dollar for the show. Hell, if they donated two dollars, we might even get a new library."

"It's a nice thought," said Sharleen.

The meeting was called to order, but it wasn't long before the night felt endless. Victor and Ivy struggled to keep their eyes open. Likewise, Sharleen and her backup were bored. She checked her watch. Lola did the same before getting up and moving to the back of the room.

Where is she going?

The board member named Peter leaned into the table microphone in front of him. "The hour is late, but we have just enough time for our Public Comment speakers." He consulted with a piece of paper. "It looks like we have two speakers tonight. Melinda

Morgan is up first. Melinda, are you here?" Peter looked out into the crowd. As he did, Sharleen decided he had the kindest face out of all the board members.

He looks like someone's dad. Probably coaches little league and volunteers to be the grill master at neighborhood cookouts.

A woman stood at the back and approached the microphone stand in front of the stage. Before she reached it, Lola intercepted and grabbed the microphone, taking it off the stand. She tried to take the microphone to where Sharleen sat in the fifth row, but the cord wasn't long enough, knocking over the stand in the process.

Realizing Lola's plan, Sharleen stood and moved fast, scrambling her way through the narrow aisle. Lola now looked like a deranged host of a daytime talk show gone wrong. The audience watched on, oblivious.

Sharleen took the microphone from Lola and held it with a firm grip, worried someone would rush in and try to take it.

Nice Peter gave her a curious look and asked, "Are you Melinda Morgan?"

"No," Sharleen said. "My name is Sharleen Vega." She cringed at the screech of feedback from the overhead sound system that filled the crowded room.

The board member with the over-styled strawberry blonde hair, Dottie, leaned forward and said into her microphone, "Ma'am, I'm sorry, but I don't see your name on the list of speakers." The shade of turquoise she wore wasn't the best color choice for her pale complexion. On her face was a sour expression that Sharleen realized was permanent, as if Dottie had been forced to eat one lemon after another all her life.

"I know," Sharleen replied, "because my name isn't on it."

"Then you'll need to wait until next year to speak." Dottie was firm.

Is she related to Holly, by any chance? A distant cousin? The wicked queen to Holly's evil princess? Had they come from the same ruthless kingdom where children suffered and afterschool program coordinators were forced into a life of servitude, with no hope for sweet victory?

Sharleen tightened her grip on the mic. "I can't do that."

From the corner of her eye, Sharleen saw a scrawny security guard start to approach her. His uniform looked far too big for him, like he was someone's little brother filling in for him for the night. The too-thin guy looked like he had second thoughts when Willie, Sylvia, and Cristina stood. Lola then stepped in his path, blocking his access to Sharleen.

"Have a seat," Lola told him. "This will only a take minute."

On stage, Dottie looked to her colleagues for help. "What is going on here?" she asked.

The others shrugged, if they even acknowledged her question at all.

The security guard took a few steps back, defeated, before leaving.

"See, our school needs your help now," Sharleen continued.

This caught Peter's attention. "Are you a teacher?"

"No," Sharleen answered. "I'm not. Not yet, anyway."

Ivy stood up and said to Sharleen, "Yes, you are." Ivy turned to the board members and said, "Yes, she is. And she's a good one, too."

Victor was on his feet then. "She's our favorite teacher," he informed the adults on stage. "She lets me dance."

Despite what the students were saying on Sharleen's behalf, Dottie was having none of it. Not an ounce of sympathy appeared on her face. The table microphone was pulled closer as if she wanted her words to be heard loud and clear. "Ma'am, this is highly inappropriate," she said in a reprimanding tone. "We have rules and protocols for a reason."

"Yes, and I respect them," Sharleen said, "but those rules and protocols are destroying a place I love."

Robert Kellis leaned forward and said into his microphone, "What school are you from?" He was a tall black man in an expensive-looking suit. He had salt and pepper hair and a genuine smile.

"I'm here from Harmonville Elementary School," she explained.

"I admire you for taking on the challenges of working at that particular school," Robert noted. "Your principal, Betty Marchant, has led a considerable charge to obtain significant support." Robert then looked directly at Dottie and said. "But unfortunately, Principal Marchant has faced considerable resistance in her—"

Rude Dottie cut him off. "Again, you're not on the list of speakers for this evening. I'm going to ask you to either sit down or leave."

The muscles in her jaw tightened. A ping of defiance spread between her shoulder blades. Sharleen locked her knees, standing firm. "I'm not leaving until you listen," she insisted.

A few people in the crowd around her offered Sharleen a smattering of applause in support of her refusal to sit down. The sound and energy of the response started to grow, gaining momentum.

Robert was adamant. "I think we should let her speak."

The other female board member, Iris, pulled her microphone to her and said, "I agree. She should be heard."

The audience encouraged this with a now rumbling roar of support.

"Fine," Dottie snapped. "You have one minute, Miss Vega." Dottie reached for a nearby stopwatch and clicked it hard. "And I'm timing you."

Sharleen took a quick breath before speaking. "Thank you," she began. "I'm here tonight because our school needs you. We are the lowest funded in the district. You say this is because of test scores or the zip code or crime in the area, but why give a school no help when it needs your help the most? I work in an afterschool program there. We're trying to put together a show for the holidays, a show the kids have worked very hard on—and some of the mothers have helped, too. But if you were to give the school more funding, we could do so much more."

Dottie interjected with, "You have thirty seconds remaining, Miss Vega."

Sharleen shot the strawberry red-haired women a look of annoyance and powered on. "These kids are talented," she said. "They deserve the same opportunities that other students in this city have. I know this because this was the school I went to myself. It's the neighborhood I come from, a place that I call home." She glanced at Victor and Ivy, who were staring at her with awe on their young faces. "I want it to be better. And it can be. Please help us. If you don't—"

Dottie was on her feet, stopwatch in hand. "Thank you, Miss Vega," she said, with a victorious smile. "You've reached your time limit. We will consider your concerns at our first board meeting next year. Now, moving on to our last agenda item for the evening—"

This time it was Dottie who was cut off from speaking. A beautiful voice was heard singing in the room. All eyes shifted to Ivy who was standing on her chair and singing an a cappella version of a song about hope.

This irritated Dottie to no end. "Can someone please ask her to stop?" she insisted. "This is a meeting, not a talent show."

In response, Ivy sang even louder. Victor stepped into the aisle and broke out into an improvised hip-hop dance. Members of the audience started to clap, creating a rhythm for both performers.

Sylvia stood up. "You can't stop her from using her voice!" Sylvia shouted above the enthusiasm of the crowd. "Just like you can't stop my son from dancing, or Miss Sharleen from being the best damn teacher we've ever had."

Lola took the microphone from Sharleen long enough to say into it, "You can't pretend like our school doesn't exist. We're not invisible. Our children deserve the same chances other kids have." She handed the mic back to Sharleen, who felt a tidal wave of emotions brewing within.

Please don't let me cry. Even though this is the most incredible thing I've ever seen or been a part of.

"Board members, I beg of you to help this school," she said. "That's all we want. Give them a library and a performing arts center and books to read. Please give my students a chance!"

Dottie waved her arms like a woman on the verge of a complete breakdown. She looked wild and furious. "This meeting is adjourned!" she shouted, her voice cracking with fury.

Robert Kellis rose out of his chair and stopped the chaos with one word, "Wait!"

The room, including Ivy, fell silent. All focus turned to him.

Sharleen watched as Robert moved from his place on stage, to the steps on the side, to the ground she stood on, and finally, he reached her. They stood, eying each other, "Miss Vega," he said, "why are you really here? Please. Tell us. I would like to know."

Sharleen saw the glimmer of empathy in his eyes as she lifted her microphone again and said into it, "I'm here because no one knows more than me the incredible gift this school is," she explained. "It's where I first learned how to play the piano and where I learned how to defend myself on the playground, and where I became the queen of chalk art. It's a part of who I am. In the last two months, these students—the entire community—have reminded me to believe in the impossible. They shouldn't be penalized because of preconceived ideas about the neighborhood they live in. Just because someone doesn't understand the challenges the families face shouldn't give them permission to punish them, just for working hard and trying to do right by their kids. Stop underestimating them ... us."

"I agree," Robert said with a small nod of approval. "You mentioned a holiday show?"

"Yes." Sharleen again directed her words to the board members. "We would love for all of you to be there, as our guests. Come see what these remarkable young people can do. I believe that once you do, you'll understand how important it is to support them ... and Principal Marchant."

Willie acted fast. Without hesitation, she was on the stage with the flyers, giving one to each board member. They each accepted one from her except for Dottie who had her arms crossed in silent refusal. Willie left one for her anyway with some words of advice, "Go with God, Dottie. He'll be happier with you for it."

Robert extended a hand to Sharleen. She shook it. "Thank you," she said to him.

"Thank you, Miss Vega," he said. "I will be there." He turned to the stage and said, "As for my fellow board members, that's up to them. As for your request for additional funding, I'll see what we can do."

The crowd showed their appreciation for Robert with a thunderous round of cheers and applause. He waited for the audience to quiet down before he looked at Ivy. She held his gaze.

"By the way, you have a beautiful voice," he said. "And a terrific teacher." Robert then turned his attention to Victor. "You're a very talented young man. I hope you get the chance to continue to use your gift."

Victor stared at Robert with reverence in his dark brown eyes and said, "Yes, sir."

Sharleen put the microphone down on her empty chair. Lola stepped in, picked it up from the seat, and replaced it on the microphone stand, which was upright again.

On impulse, Sharleen walked to the edge of the stage. There, she looked Dottie in the eye from where she stood and said, "For whatever it's worth ... I forgive you."

Dottie continued to fume, radiating an intense rage. Seeing how angry Dottie was made Sharleen take pause.

"I hope someday you can find joy ... especially in helping others."

May I never become so jaded and ungrateful that I turn into this woman or anything like her.

Sharleen turned away from Dottie and the other board members and reached for Ivy's hand. Together, they headed toward the main entrance, along with the rest of the audience. She spotted Jake immediately. He was standing in the back with both hands dug deep into the front pockets of his faded blue jeans. She approached him with a smile.

"Wow," he beamed. "All I can say is, wow." He turned to his daughter and said, "I'm proud of both of you."

"Thank you, daddy," the ten-year-old replied. "Can we stop for ice cream on the way home?"

"You bet we can. I think you've both earned a double scoop tonight."

They stepped into the lobby. Sharleen noticed Holly lingering nearby within earshot.

Cristina stepped in Sharleen's direction. Sylvia, Lola, Willie, and Victor followed. "What you said in there ... it meant a lot," Cristina said. She reached out and hugged Sharleen. "Thank you."

It was Sylvia's turn next. "Sharleen, you're the best thing to ever happen to our school. What you've done for us and for our kids … we owe you big time."

Holly's cell phone buzzed. Sharleen saw her answer the call, their eyes meeting briefly in the process.

"I just hope they listened," said Lola.

"Well, if they didn't, we'll come back again," Sharleen vowed. "We'll keep coming back until they do."

Holly suddenly stepped forward, taking all of them by surprise. She handed her cell phone to Sharleen.

Before Holly spoke, Sharleen already knew something was wrong. She sensed it, felt it in her pulsing veins, quickened with an instant dash of pure adrenaline.

"Sharleen, something's happened," Holly said. "At the school. Something bad. Betty's on the phone." Holly took a breath and blinked back tears. "I really think you should speak to her."

Slowly, Sharleen placed the phone to her ear. She took a deep breath, preparing.

And hoping.

EIGHTEEN

Fire

SHARLEEN FELT LIKE she was moving in a perpetual state of slow motion. Like she was stuck in a universe where everything was forced to move at half the speed they were used to. The surge of fear and adrenaline had left her wired and restless. Too much was happening around here. Her senses were on overdrive, overloaded by all that surrounded her.

Feeling lost, she wandered through the scene, trying to process everything she was seeing and hearing. And smelling. That strong odor of smoke and fire reached into her mind and shook loose the vivid memory of standing at the gate staring up at her family home engulfed by flames, knowing her parents were inside and most likely dead. The same overwhelming sense of numbness was back. It terrified her to feel it again.

Sharleen knew her feet were moving, but they were doing so as if they'd switched into an automatic mode, guiding her from person to person, forcing her to see the shock and grief. Wondering if she was stumbling her way through a maze of sad, haunting images and traveling through someone else's life, she continued to move, stopping along the way to stare and try to decipher the scenery before her.

First, she saw Jake. He stood underneath a redwood tree holding Ivy, who was staring at the building with a look of terror and sadness. Jake looked at Sharleen and she saw tears in his eyes. It was the first time he'd ever appeared truly helpless. His vulnerability only made Sharleen ache inside even more.

She moved. There was Willie, watching the firefighters do their job. She even patted one on the back before he headed toward the building, hose in hand. While Willie was trying to appear brave, Sharleen knew her breaking point was only seconds away.

Close by, Sylvia, Lola, and Cristina, huddled together. Sylvia's hands were clasped together in prayer. Cristina was sobbing, comforted by Lola's strong arm around her. Lola looked in Sharleen's direction. Their eyes met in the haze, speaking silently. The exchange between them was intense and rife with sorrow. Finally, Lola spoke and her words cut through the thick air. "It's going to be all right," she promised.

The flashing, circling lights of the fire trucks caught Sharleen's attention next. She watched their movement, feeling somewhat hypnotized and mesmerized by the constant motion. Dazed, she moved on.

From a distance, Sharleen watched while Betty spoke to a concerned news reporter who was preparing to go live from the scene. The female camera operator was setting up the shot, headphones covering her ears.

"I understand," the reporter said to the principal. "I'm a mother. I can't imagine something like this happening to their school."

What exactly did happen?

As if he were able to read her mind, Jake found her. He touched her arm. This made her stop moving, bringing a much-needed stillness to her body. She froze in her steps and looked at him for answers.

Please tell me what's going on.

"It's only part of the multipurpose room," he explained. His voice sounded like it was rolling down a long tunnel before it reached her. She tried to concentrate on what he was saying, his words. "It was the stage lights. The wiring." Still feeling like she was standing in the middle of a bad, smokey dream, Sharleen nodded in response, finding herself speechless.

What can I say at this moment? What words could possibly change what's happened?

"The rest of the school wasn't touched," Jake said. "The building is still standing."

Sharleen turned as she heard someone nearby say, "This could've been so much worse."

We could've been inside. Trapped.

Although the fire had been put out, smoke continued to billow from the multipurpose room, as though sending out a distress signal, messaging for help.

"The damage is considerable," Betty was telling the reporter.

"What can people do to help?" the reporter asked.

Pray. That's all we can do, pray.

The memory wouldn't let Sharleen go. It taunted and plagued her as she stood in the parking lot, damp from panic and sweat. She remembered screaming when she saw the house on fire. She'd begged anyone who would listen to please save her parents. *They don't deserve to die.* She knew she was their only hope, their only chance for survival.

It was then Sharleen felt someone tugging at her sweatshirt. She looked down into Ivy's bewildered eyes.

"What are we going to do now, Miss Sharleen?" Ivy's cheeks were stained with tears.

"Whatever we have to," Sharleen said. "It's going to be okay."

Someone was crying. The sound found Sharleen, calling to her. She turned in its direction.

Victor was alone. Like Sharleen, he was watching the whirlwind of motion as it unfolded around him like a wind-torn map. Tears were streaming down his face, the glimmer of them caught in the reflective lights of the fire trucks.

Without hesitation, Sharleen went and kneeled before him. Victor's small body poured into the space inside her open, outstretched arms. Ivy was there, too. Both students clung to Sharleen, sobbing and scared. Within seconds, Sharleen was crying too. In the dark, she held the children close to her, reassuring them with sounds and closeness that they were safe. That it was okay to show their sorrow to the world. Victor's body trembled as he wept. She tightened her hold on him, feeling as if she were somehow hugging herself.

Morning came early. Wide awake, Sharleen sat at her kitchen table, drinking coffee and blindly eating the gumdrops Professor Richter had gifted her. The edge of dawn crept through the window, covering the table with splashes of struggling sun. Outside, the city of Harmonville was waking up to face another day. For so many, it would feel like just another day. It was Friday, which might instantly improve many moods, even before coffee was brewed, eggs were cracked, and shower faucets reached for.

Yet, for Sharleen, nothing felt normal. Already, there was a cruelty to the day that hadn't existed before.

Hoping for some form of comfort, she looked at the Christmas tree, at the photo of her parents. She turned in her chair and glanced at the open but still packed boxes of cows.

Lita, I have to make a very difficult choice. But I know it's a decision that you would bless.

At that moment, Sharleen knew what she had to do. There was no other choice. She stood up, finished her last bit of lukewarm coffee in two gulps, and then walked into her bedroom. She stood in the doorway for a second, waiting for the last bit of hesitation to disappear.

Now's not the time to second guess yourself.

With a shaky hand, Sharleen retrieved the white velvet ring box from the drawer in her nightstand and slipped it into the pocket of her jeans.

Back in the living room, she reached for her backpack, more out of habit than for a specific purpose. She stopped, staring inside at the familiar sight of the urns she'd carried on her back for the last seven years, day in and day out. They'd been her secret all that time, giving solace to her constant state of sorrow.

No more.

Inhaling a deep breath, she reached into the backpack and took the urns out, placing them on the kitchen table.

She picked up the bag and slid her arms through the shoulder straps.

Instantly, the backpack was much lighter.

Sharleen was ready to go.

In her heart, there was a tiny flicker in the form of newfound hope.

NINETEEN

Sacrifice

THE DAY WAS cold and gray. Yet the holiday decorations helped bring some cheer to the town square. As she walked through the park, Sharleen spotted Jake sitting in the gazebo. She noticed his expression brightened when he saw her approaching. He stood to greet her. He was dressed for the temperature, in a black wool coat, a sweater, and jeans.

She joined him inside the wooden structure. They embraced, and he planted a welcome kiss on her cheek.

It's so good to see him, even though it's only been hours since we said good night.

"Thank you for meeting me here," she said.

He smells good. Like happiness. Like love.

"Of course," he said. She slipped off her backpack and put it on the ground. They sat on one of the wooden benches, shoulder to shoulder. Sharleen shivered a little. This prompted Jake to wrap an arm around her. "You said it was important. What's going on?"

On the bus ride, Sharleen had planned every word she was going to say. Now that she was sitting next to him, all that preparation seemed pointless because she found herself searching for the right way to ask for his help.

She took a calming breath.

Here we go.

"What I want to talk to you about might sound crazy at first," she began. "So listen with an open mind."

"After what happened last night, I don't think anything sounds crazy anymore," he said.

"I agree. Okay … I know you're a contractor and a good one from what you've told me."

"Yup," he said with a nod. "I have been for eleven years." He paused. "What does my job have to do with this conversation?"

"I was just getting to that," she explained. "In your professional opinion, what would it take to fix the multipurpose room in time for the show?"

There, I said it.

Jake gave her a look of disbelief. His expression changed when he realized she was serious. "Other than a miracle?" He paused. "A lot of people."

"And money?"

"Definitely," he said. "And probably some support from the city."

"What kind of support?" she asked.

"Help with red tape and permits," he said. "That sort of thing. Rebuilding city property isn't an easy thing to do by any means."

"How much would it take?" Sharleen asked. "Money, I mean."

He gave this some thought. "What, you want an exact amount?"

She nodded. "Yes."

"It's hard to say without inspecting the place first," Jake explained. "I have no idea what the smoke and water damage is like. I'd have to get inside and take a look around."

"But is it possible?" There was urgency in her voice, even a tinge of desperation. "In eleven days?"

Jake pulled away from her and stood up. "What are you getting at, Sharleen?"

She stared up at him, pleading with her eyes. "I just want to know if there's a chance … is it possible?"

"I'm scared to say yes because of the wild look in your eyes," he said. "But … yes. It's possible."

She stood and joined him. "Good. Then let's make it happen."

He held up a hand of caution. "Whoa, let's slow down here for a second. What you're talking about isn't as easy as you think, no matter how noble of a gesture it is."

"It's not about me at all, Jake," she insisted.

"I know that. And I admire your gumption … but this is a big ask."

"It is," she agreed. "In fact, this feels bigger than anything I've ever experienced or done before."

"Same goes for me," he said.

"But it feels necessary. It feels like something I have to do … or at least try to do … with everything I have."

"Listen," he said. "I'm on board with you, but I'm worried. What if we promise the kids that we can do this and then something happens, and we can't deliver?"

He has a good point. I can't disappoint the students. Or even the neighborhood, for that matter.

"I realize that's a possibility," she conceded, "but I truly believe it's a risk we should take."

He wrapped his arms around her. "Together?" he asked.

She kissed him softly and said, "Is there any other way?"

Jake's eyes brightened as if an idea had struck him. "Hey, do you have plans this morning?" He sounded excited, almost giddy.

"Other than studying for finals, no. Did you have something in mind?"

"I'd love to warm up by making out with you for an hour, but since that's probably out of the question, I'd settle for pancakes."

"Pancakes," she repeated with a giggle. "Yum. I will definitely take you up on that. I'm starving."

"I know a great place not far from here. We can have breakfast and talk through the details of this idea of yours. Maybe figure out what our next steps are."

"Yes," she said, with an enthusiastic nod. "Let's go."

Sharleen turned to grab her backpack, but Jake touched the sleeve of her jacket and stopped her.

"By the way, I noticed you're carrying a much lighter load," he said. "I'm proud of you."

She turned back to him and saw love in his eyes. "It's not easy," she confessed. "I'm not ready to let go. I never will be." She reached for his hand. "But I am ready to move forward."

"With me?" he asked, with a flash of vulnerability in his dark eyes.

"Yes, of course. And don't think I missed your reference to making out."

"I was wondering if you'd missed that completely, or if you were ignoring it," he joked.

"That needs to happen," she whispered.

She had his full attention. "Oh, yeah?"

"Yeah," Sharleen said. "And soon."

"I'm a patient man," he reminded her.

"Jake, you're the best thing to have happened to me," she said, feeling warm tears fill the corners of her eyes. "I wouldn't be able to make it through all of this without you. I hope you know that."

"I do," he said, with an adorable grin. "But it's still very nice to hear."

The quaint coffee shop was small but not very crowded. It had a homespun atmosphere, complete with country music playing faintly in the background. Jake and Sharleen sat at a table, not far from the front door.

"We must have just missed the breakfast rush," Jake said, as they glanced over the menus they'd been handed.

"You did," the upbeat, tattooed waitress said, as she filled their cups with hot coffee. "You two know what you want, or do you need a minute to decide."

"You can order for both of us," Sharleen said. "Since you've been here before."

"All right. We'll both have the Sunrise Special and orange juice."

"How do you want your eggs?" the waitress asked.

"Over medium for me," Jake answered.

"I'll have mine scrambled," Sharleen said.

"Toast, muffins, or pancakes?"

"Pancakes," Jake and Sharleen said, in unison with a youthful sense of glee.

Jake waited until the waitress was out of earshot before he spoke again. "I have to be honest about something."

Concerned, Sharleen felt a tickle of tension in her body. "Tell me."

"There's something you and I are not going to be able to avoid no matter how hard we try … at least if we're planning on living in Harmonville for the rest of our lives, which I'm assuming at this point we are."

She stared at him, confused. "I'm not sure what you mean."

"This town isn't very big," he continued.

"I don't know … it seems large enough to be divided."

"I was married for twelve years before we met. My wife and I…"

"Penny," she said, permitting him to say her name.

"Penny and I … we went to many of the places I'll end up taking you to … there's no way around it really … I mean, of course it will be different when we go because you're a different person … I just don't want it to feel … weird … for you."

She smiled at him, took a sip of her black coffee, and said, "I appreciate you looking out for me and my feelings, but I get it, Jake. You had a life, long before we met. In fact, we both did."

He raised an eyebrow. "You were married, too?"

"No, nothing like that." She said, followed by a short laugh. "To tell you the truth, I don't have a whole lot of experience in the love department."

"I don't believe that," he said. "I mean, look at you. You're a knockout."

"That's very sweet of you to say." She took a deeper look into Jake's eyes before she continued. "I had a high school boyfriend, but he got a big scholarship and was scouted to play college basketball, so he moved away and broke my heart. He didn't even say goodbye unless you count the text he sent me from his new dorm room. But then he got injured, and he lost the scholarship, married a really mean woman, and now he's a DJ at bar mitzvahs and weddings."

Jake grinned, seeming to find amusement in Sharleen's shared memory. "I'm no good at basketball," he said. "So there's no chance of me leaving anytime soon."

"That's okay." She smiled. "You're good at other things."

"I used to dream about becoming a chef ... when I was younger, I mean."

"Why didn't you?"

"Because I met Penny and we fell in love," he explained. "She got pregnant and I knew I needed to do the right thing and take care of us. Her father was a contractor and took me under his wing. Taught me everything he knew. Then Ivy came along and thoughts about being a chef went away."

"You do realize it's something you can still do," Sharleen said. "If it's a question of taking care of Ivy, I can help."

"She's crazy about you. So am I."

Heat flamed her cheeks. Overwhelmed by Jake's romantic words, she reached for her coffee cup again. "Then please don't feel weird about taking me to familiar places," she said. "I mean it. It's not a big deal."

"You know what I'm really looking forward to?"

In the distance, Sharleen spotted their waitress heading in their direction carrying two plates, "Pancakes," she said, and as if on cue, her empty stomach grumbled.

"Yes. Always pancakes ... and making new memories together."

"Let's make a deal. I think you and I need a lot of new memories ... I know they won't all be good ones, but let's aim high."

Jake nodded. "Deal."

Their food arrived.

"This looks amazing," Sharleen marveled.

"Only the best for us from here on out," Jake said, with a dimpled smile.

Sharleen picked up the bottle of warm syrup. "By the way, what were you like in high school?"

"Quiet," he said. "And moody. I read too much poetry and lived inside comic books. But I could raise hell on a skateboard."

After saying goodbye and promising they'd meet up later to take Ivy out to dinner, Sharleen made the five-block walk to her next destination. Once she reached the gaudy pawn shop, she stared at the bars on the front windows, the bulletproof front door, and the rotating obnoxious sign protruding from the roof like a con-stant waving yellow and red hand.

Doubts danced through her mind as she stood there on the curb, contemplating. She'd done some research on her phone while riding the bus earlier, knowing she would get a decent amount for the ring.

But will it be enough? It has to be.

Finally, Sharleen reached for the front door and pulled it open. She stepped inside and was greeted with a warm blast of radiated air. Within seconds she was sweating, not just because the establishment was so stuffy, but because she felt the magnitude of what she was about to do.

She walked the length of the small store and approached the counter, where a woman wearing a beautiful and colorful ka an stood. The expression on the woman's face didn't change when Sharleen said, "Good afternoon."

From her pocket, Sharleen took out the boxed ring. She placed it on the counter, noticing a slight tremble in her hand.

"I'd like to pawn this," she said.

Because I have no other choice.

TWENTY

We Take Care of Our Own

Now that her backpack was lighter, Sharleen was able to move quicker. This liberation was especially evident when she stepped off the bus later that day, anxious to get to the school and receive an update on the damage. Also, a new rehearsal space for her students had to be found, and fast.

I need to see Joyce. She'll have some ideas on where we can rehearse.

After Sharleen exited the bus through the rear door, she began her brief two-block journey, carrying one bookbag, instead of the usual two. The temperature had dropped even more since she'd spent the morning with Jake. The stinging air felt like ice against her skin. Still, she soldiered on.

At the next intersection, she crossed the street with purpose. There was something she needed to do.

Seconds later, she reached the front gate of her old house. There, she stopped. She stood in silence, staring at her past. A range of mixed emotions filled her heart, a bittersweet combination of sorrow and relief.

It's just a house now. Nothing more. I'm taking all of the memories with me.

For a brief moment, Sharleen imagined her parents standing on the porch. They looked happy. Her father was waving at her. Her mother was smiling.

"I love you both," she said to the vision. "Always."

Behind her parents, Alma suddenly appeared. She joined her daughter and son-in-law, standing in the middle and locking arms with them momentarily.

"*Lita?*" Sharleen said. "I miss you so much." She was aware that she was crying then.

I look like an insane person, standing on the sidewalk bawling my eyes out and talking to ghosts.

In response, Alma blew her granddaughter a kiss.

"We love you, *m'ija*," Alma said.

And then, they were gone.

Sharleen remained still for a moment, both shaken by the imagined moment, but grateful for it at the same time.

They were saying goodbye to me. They were giving me permission to move on. I know they were.

Sharleen turned away from the house, and took a few steps before stopping to glance back.

This is where the sadness belongs. Behind me.

Sharleen counted the cracks in the sidewalk as she continued down the street. Up ahead, the smell of coffee brewing emanated from the Cuban coffee shop. Somewhere in the distance, a church bell chimed. An old woman stepped out of the corner market, carrying grocery sacks in her hands. Mothers and fathers were walking to the park, pushing strollers as they passed by.

This is home. This is where I belong.

As Sharleen reached the outer edges of the playground and the first post in the chain-link fence, she squinted to make sure her eyes weren't playing a trick on her.

What is he doing here?

Standing in the exact spot that her father used to stand when he would greet her each day and marvel at her new chalk art creation was Jake. He smiled when he saw her. She quickened her step, picking up her pace, anxious.

Please don't let whatever he's about to tell me be more bad news. My heart can't take it. Not today.

"Fancy running into you here," she greeted. "This is a pleasant surprise, seeing you twice in one day."

"Three if you count dinner tonight," he said with a wink.

"I'm counting. I'm counting," she joked. "I've been looking forward to it since we said goodbye this morning."

Sharleen extended her hand. The book bag was dangling from her wrist. "Here," she said. "It's all I could get, so I hope it's enough."

He took the bag from her with some reluctance in the way he moved. "What is this?"

"It's what you said we need to make the impossible possible," she explained, being cryptic on purpose.

Jake let out an audible gasp once peering inside the book bag. "I'm afraid to ask this, but did you rob a bank? Are you a fugitive right now?"

"I didn't rob a bank," she said, lightly slapping his arm in jest. "Although the thought did cross my mind, but only for a second."

"What did you do?" Jake asked, sounding shocked. "Where did you get this cash?"

"You said we needed money to rebuild, so I got some."

"But this is a lot of money, Sharleen."

"If there's anything left over, I would love some dance shoes for my kids and a piano tuner."

"I think we can make that happen," he said, "But first, I want you to meet a few of our closest friends."

"What are you talking about?"

Jake started to walk again. Curious, Sharleen quickly followed.

"Come on," he urged. "There are some people who want to see you."

They stepped into the first section of the school parking lot. Sharleen glanced up, catching a few waves from the rippling American flag snapping in the wintry air.

Then she saw them. There was a large crowd gathered near the main entrance of the building. Immediately, at the sight of so many familiar faces, Sharleen collided with Jake, bursting into tears. He reached out and steadied her.

As they reached their friends, Sharleen stared at their faces, taking each one in and letting their presence fill a space in her heart.

Betty was standing front and center, with the beautiful crowd behind her, which included Maisy, Willie, Sylvia, Lola, Cristina, Joyce, Victor, Ivy, Raquel, Camilla, and the other students who were in the show. Beyond that, people from the community had joined the cause, many of them strangers to Sharleen. In all, there were more than a hundred people there to greet her and Jake.

"Jake called me this morning and told me your idea about rebuilding," Betty said. "He also told me you have a fondness for pancakes, as do I."

"Guilty on both counts," Sharleen said, wiping her eyes with the back of her gloved hand. "All of you are here to help?"

"Yes, we are," Sylvia said. "Because we take care of our own."

"Thank you, everyone," said Sharleen, still overwhelmed by the show of solidarity. "It means so much that you're here."

"Where else would we be?" Lola said. "Nowhere else but right by your side, girl."

Ivy ran to her father and wrapped her arms around him. "Daddy, are we really going to rebuild the stage?"

"We're certainly going to try," he promised.

"That's all we can do," Betty said. "Each and every day."

"Amen," added Sylvia.

"Through tragedy can come a blessing," Betty concluded. "Now, enough conversation, we have a lot of work to do and a show to put on."

The crowd responded to Betty with a loud, beautiful cheer.

Victor broke through the crowd and rushed to Sharleen's side. He took her hand into his. "Miss Sharleen, my mom said you're going to help me find a dance class to go to. Thank you."

"Does this mean you're coming back to the show?" she asked. "Finally?"

"Yes," he said. "I can't wait." His smile lifted her spirits even more.

Jake reached out and pulled Sharleen aside. He lowered his voice to a whisper. "It just dawned on me … the money … I know how you got it."

"Do you?"

He nodded. "Your grandmother's ring…"

She held his inquisitive stare, unable to look away. "You are correct," she said. "Right now my grandmother's ring is sitting in a pawn shop downtown. It was a sacrifice worth making. I mean, look at how many people are here."

From the corner of her eye, Sharleen saw two more people approaching the crowd.

Holly was dressed more casually than usual, and her dark hair was down, whipping across her face in the chilly wind. Her cheeks were flushed from the cold. Obedient George was trailing behind her, dressed in a pair of overalls and a flannel shirt. He was carrying a shovel, for what purpose, Sharleen didn't know. He was like a scarecrow that had magically come to life, ready to be put to work.

There was a humble expression in Holly's eyes when she came face-to-face with Sharleen. "Is there room for two more?" she asked.

Sharleen nodded, offered Holly a genuine smile, and said, "Always."

TWENTY-ONE

Rebuilding

THAT AFTERNOON, JAKE announced he'd be working late that night, explaining to Sharleen about the considerable amount of planning that needed to happen for the rebuild of the multipurpose room to not only be safe but for it to be completed on time. He'd quickly assembled a crew to oversee the complex project, but the team needed to meet to discuss, troubleshoot, and strategize.

"There's a lot to be done and not a lot of time to make it happen," he said. "The clock is ticking and we all feel it."

Sharleen offered to stay with Ivy, to make sure she ate dinner, finished her homework, and got to bed at a decent hour.

That evening, Sharleen and Ivy sat at the dining table in Ivy's house with an open box of pizza positioned between them, and glasses of iced tea. Their paper plates were covered with hot slices of pepperoni pizza. Ivy wasted no time consuming her portion, claiming once again pizza was her favorite thing to eat. Next to ice cream, of course.

Once Ivy finished eating, she looked at Sharleen with a curious expression. "Do you like being here with us … in our house?"

Sharleen put down her almost-finished slice of pizza, reached for her napkin, and said, "What do you mean?"

At first, Ivy seemed hesitant to share her feelings but then powered through. "My dad said you don't have a family anymore. He said you were all alone," Ivy said. "It makes me sad when I think about that. About how you don't have a mom either."

At once, a lump formed in Sharleen's throat, knowing that tears were rising within.

This young girl has already known so much grief in her life. I have to remember she was so much younger than I was when she lost her mom. I can't imagine what she's feeling, what she goes through. To not have a mom at such a young age.

Sharleen took a quick sip of iced tea before responding. "I used to be sad … very sad, actually … but you and your father have brought a lot of joy into my life," she explained. "And I'm thankful for that."

Ivy gave this some thought, nodding her head. "I think you did the same thing for us."

Sharleen smiled at her dinner date. "I hope so."

Silent for a moment, it was clear to Sharleen that Ivy had a lot to say, a lot she wanted to share. "I like having you here with me," Ivy said.

"You do?"

"Yes, my dad is always smiling when you're around or when he talks about you he acts very goofy sometimes." Ivy let out a giggle. "He's like a big puppy dog. I told him so. I told him he was a silly puppy dog dad."

Sharleen laughed, too. "It's okay to be goofy if you're feeling happy."

Ivy's giggle disappeared and her facial expression turned more serious. "But he wasn't happy for a long time because he missed my mom," she said. Sharleen thought she saw tears in Ivy's eyes. "I miss her, too. Do you think I always will?"

Sharleen got up from her chair and went to Ivy, kneeling next to her. Behind her, the Christmas tree lights blinked and twinkled, casting a beautiful rainbow of colors on them. "Yes, but that's okay," she said. "And it's okay to get sad about it sometimes, too."

Ivy looked into Sharleen's eyes. "But if I get sad, I can come to you and tell you, right?"

"Of course." Sharleen's heart melted.

Ivy's infectious grin was back. "Sometimes I think you're magical." It felt like a secret that was being shared.

I've been called many things in my life, but magical … this is a first. If I were magical, I wouldn't have finals next week.

"Me?" she said, touched by the thought. "That's very sweet of you to say, Ivy, but I'm not magical."

"But since we met you, a lot of the sadness has gone away," Ivy explained. "And how my dad is so different now. And how you help me to sing."

"I want you to sing because you have a beautiful voice," Sharleen said. "I was scared to play the piano a long time ago and I'm so glad I didn't let that fear stop me."

"I like it when you play. You look so happy when you do." Ivy took a breath before adding, "But you look even happier when you're here at our house."

Sharleen stood up. She closed the lid on the pizza box, then collected their empty paper plates and glasses. As she walked into the kitchen to find a place to throw the garbage, she said, "I like being here with you and your dad."

Once Sharleen returned from the kitchen, Ivy said, "Maybe you'll stay here forever … I mean, even when Christmas is over. Do you think you will?"

Sharleen moved closer. "Would you like that?"

Her smile widened. "Yes, yes I would." Her little head bobbed up and down, tears disappearing.

Sharleen moved into the living room and Ivy followed. They found a comfy spot on the couch and sat together.

"I hope you know … I would never try to take your mom's place, Ivy. I couldn't do that, no matter how hard I tried. And I wouldn't want to."

Ivy was quiet for a moment, most likely processing their conversation. Her eyes brightened a little when she said, "You and my mom are very different." She turned to Sharleen. "I really think I can love you both."

Sharleen tried her hardest to stay awake long enough to greet Jake when he got home, but exhaustion won the battle. Shortly after tucking Ivy into bed for the night, she crawled onto the sofa and was fast asleep within seconds.

The next thing she knew, Jake was standing over her and whispering her name.

She wondered if he was a part of her dream. He certainly looked like a dark-haired prince who'd fought the creatures of the night to be by her side when she woke.

"You have beautiful eyes," she said, without thinking and not fully awake.

What did I just say to him? This isn't a dream. Where am I?

"Do you want me to drive you home?" he asked.

Oh, that's right. I don't live here. I have an apartment filled with porcelain cows.

She sat up, yawned, and stretched. "What time is it?"

"It's late, after eleven."

"I tried to stay awake, but I guess I was really tired."

"No need to explain," he said. "Do you want to go home? Sleep in your own bed?"

Sharleen gave him a look. "Or I could stay," she suggested.

She could see a look of contemplation on his face. "That's fine," he said.

She sat up when she realized he was heading out of the room. "Where are you going?"

"To get you a pillow and a blanket," he explained. "I'll be right back."

Just my luck. This prince is a perfect gentleman.

Arriving at the school the next morning, she was impressed by the organized way things were getting done. This was evident by the handwritten signs taped to the front windows, offering volunteers information about where to go for what. As she walked through the main entrance of the building, passed the trophy case, and found her way to the unofficial hub, she couldn't help but feel deeply inspired.

Down the hallway, more handmade signs were everywhere, prompting volunteers to follow a specific path. She passed many friendly faces who all looked like Harmonville Elementary School was the only place in the world they wanted to be.

"Thank you so much for being here," Sharleen said to every person she saw.

The signs ended, and she entered a room where the final hand-drawn arrow was pointing at. Inside, someone had converted one of the larger classrooms into a central meeting area, a place where the volunteers could safely store their belongings or take a quick break when needed.

Even though the hour was early, Joyce was already working hard to set up a long table for snacks, juice boxes, and bottles of water, which were stacked in almost every corner Sharleen had passed, inside and out.

"Good morning," Sharleen greeted her with a smile.

"Oh, Sharleen, am I happy to see you," Joyce said, rattled but exuding her usual optimism and warmth. "There's so much to do."

"Did you set all of this up in here? This is great."

"I did," Joyce said. "Luckily we have a couple of classrooms that aren't in use."

"Where did all of these snacks and stuff come from?" she asked, in awe. "There's so many."

Holly entered the classroom at that moment with her cell phone to her ear. She was dressed in jeans and a comfy sweatshirt. Her long hair was pulled back away from her face with a folded red bandana. "I had them donated," she explained. "I'm working on getting us lunch now ... for the rest of the weekend. I'll be right back." She returned to the hallway.

Joyce looked at Sharleen with a secretive smile. "Isn't it nice to see Holly using her ... charm ... for a good cause?"

"It is a nice change, that's for sure."

Joyce reached into a large recyclable grocery bag and pulled out a dark linen tablecloth. "Want to help me set up the food area? The volunteers will need a break soon and I want to be ready for them when they do. They're all working so hard."

"Of course."

They went to work and within minutes, Joyce stood back to inspect the end result. She looked pleased.

"I never thought I'd see this happen," she said. "In all the years I've worked at this school, I've never seen the neighborhood come together like this. It really touches my heart."

"Yes," Sharleen said. "I know exactly what you mean."

"This is all your doing," Joyce said, glowing with gratitude. "If you hadn't come back when you did..."

George suddenly appeared in the doorway. In his thin arms, he carried a large wicker basket. It was overflowing with dance shoes in all sizes. Sharleen nearly applauded when she saw them.

"Joyce, what should I do with these? They just arrived," he explained.

"Put them over there in the corner so they're out of the way," Joyce instructed.

He placed the basket in an empty spot. Sharleen went to the basket and picked up a few shoes. They were of exceptional quality, the best.

"Where did these come from?" she asked, stunned.

"A store downtown donated them," George explained. "Holly's been calling businesses and asking them to help. Everyone has been saying yes, but, then again, it's pretty hard to say no to her when she wants something."

"So many people have been donating stuff all morning," Joyce said. "It's like a miracle. I had to open another classroom just for storage and it's already full, wall to wall. Isn't it wonderful?"

"This is incredible," Sharleen said. "Joyce, do you know what was donated exactly?"

"All of those supplies you wanted and then some. It's like you wished for it and it happened."

Don't tell Ivy that or she really will think I possess some form of unearthly powers.

"There're costumes, stage lights, lumber, a lot of cans of paint, Christmas trees, and several boxes of candy canes," George said. He peered out the classroom window and said, "Look! More stuff just arrived."

Sharleen followed George's gaze to the window. In the lot, a delivery truck was parked. From the back of it, two people in matching T-shirts and baseball caps were unloading an upright piano.

"Is that a piano?" Sharleen couldn't believe her own eyes.

Joyce joined them at the window. "Yes, and it looks new, too."

A thought struck Sharleen. "Joyce, is someone keeping track of everything that's being donated?"

"Willie has been keeping a very detailed list."

As proof of that, they saw Willie appear in the parking lot, where she was greeting the two movers. They watched Willie shake their hands and then walked with them as they wheeled the instrument toward the building. Willie carried a clipboard, writing while walking.

"Good heavens," Joyce said. "Where in the heck are we going to store that thing? The multipurpose room won't be ready for a few more days."

"We'll find a place," Sharleen said with determination.

Later, Sharleen searched the building for Jake. She found him standing just outside the gutted multipurpose room. Through a window in the double doors, Sharleen could see his crew hard at work inside, but it was clear there was still so much to do. A symphony of power tools could be heard filtering through the air.

Jake had something in his hands that looked like a blueprint. He was studying it, eyes cast on the paper, concentrating. He smiled when he glanced up and saw Sharleen. She handed him a paper cup of coffee.

"I thought you might need this," she said. "And I think I made it the way you like … two sugars and a splash of cream."

"Thank you. This is perfect."

"They're so many people here, Jake. I can't believe it. Everywhere I look, someone is cleaning something or painting or building."

"The turnout of volunteers is unlike anything I've ever seen."

"Do you think we'll actually be able to pull this off?" Sharleen asked.

"It's too early to tell, but I'm definitely feeling optimistic."

"So am I," she said. "Someone donated a brand new piano to us. It's in the girls' bathroom at the moment because it was the only empty space we could find, but it's beautiful."

"So are you," he said.

She smiled and gave him a quick kiss. "You're not so bad yourself, mister."

A voice interrupted their intimate moment. It was George. "Sharleen?" he said, an embarrassed expression on his face and his blue eyes to the ground. "So sorry for interrupting the two of you, but Betty needs you outside. There's a news crew here and they want to interview you."

"Oh, no," she said. "Looking like this?"

"Think of the children," Jake chided. "Do it for them. Besides, I have a feeling the camera will love you."

"Thank you for the vote of confidence, but this is why I prefer working behind the scenes. I don't need the attention or the glory."

"Go," Jake said. "Speak from the heart."

George was at her side as she moved toward the main exit. "Sharleen, I was wondering if I could ask you something?"

"Sure. What is it?"

"Do you think I could be in charge of coordinating the costumes for the show?" She could hear the nervousness in his voice.

Sharleen stopped in her tracks. George then did the same. "Is that something you really want to do? It's a big responsibility."

"Yes. My grandmother was a professional seamstress and costume designer. She used to create costumes for operas. She taught me a lot about it when I was young. I think I still remember some of it."

"That would be wonderful, George," she said. "Thank you for volunteering for such an important task."

They started to walk again.

"It will be nice to do something for someone other than Holly for a change."

Sharleen pushed open the door and stepped out into the cold air. She saw George shiver in response to the icy temperature. "Yeah, about that," she said. "It's okay to stand on your own and be your own person, George."

"I don't help her for me," he explained. "I do it for her. Otherwise, she would be lost without me."

He has a point.

Sure enough, a news crew was set up and ready to go live, planning to broadcast directly from the school parking lot. The beautiful news reporter was getting a touch-up from a makeup person when Sharleen arrived.

I have to stand next to her? She looks like a supermodel.

Although Sharleen knew Betty was exhausted, the principal looked professional in a dark blue pants suit and silk blouse. Her hair was styled to perfection and her lipstick looked flawless. "It's been a long week," she said to Sharleen. "I don't think there's any rest in sight for either of us."

"That's okay," Sharleen said. "We can catch up on sleep later."

"Spoken like a true hero," the news reporter said, joining them. "I'm Tammy."

"And I'm no hero," Sharleen said.

"Sure you are," Tammy insisted. "Just ask anyone who's here today."

"Wait," Sharleen said. "This isn't about me."

"She's right," Betty agreed. "As much as Sharleen has done for our school, and our community, this is about the students. Can we please keep the focus on them?"

The reporter still looked clueless and hopelessly sentimental. "You're right and we will. But our viewers want a hero. Trust me. It will inspire them to do even more for you."

Someone nearby said, "We're going live in, five ... four ... three ... two ... one."

Sharleen watched as an instant smile flashed across the face of the tall blonde. "I'm Tammy Sanderson coming to you live from Harmonville Elementary School, where local community members have rallied together in the aftermath of a fire just days before a scheduled performance of a holiday variety show, the first of its kind to be performed in the long history of this school—the oldest grade school in our city. I'm joined today by Principal Betty Marchant and afterschool program coordinator Sharleen Vega, who is also the director of the planned production."

Sharleen felt a wild kaleidoscope of thoughts and emotions overcome her. *What's happening right now? I feel like I just left my body and I'm watching a scene from someone else's life. Betty looks so poised and together.*

Tammy's sugar-sweet voice interrupted Sharleen's thoughts when she asked Betty a question. "Principal Marchant, how do you describe all that's happening today at your beloved school?"

Betty smiled, looked into the camera, and replied, "It's a blessing, really it is."

The microphone suddenly appeared just below Sharleen's face. "Miss Vega, is there anything you'd like to add?" Tammy prompted.

"These remarkable students deserve a fair chance to shine," she said. "Please help them and this school if you can. We're grateful to everyone who has been donating items and supplies and their time and energy. This truly is a group effort."

After they survived the live interview and said their goodbyes to a weepy Tammy Sanderson, Joyce was there to urge Betty and Sharleen back inside.

"It's lunchtime," she said. "I want to make sure both of you get something to eat. You need some nutrition to keep your strength up."

"You always take such good care of everyone," Betty said. "Really, Joyce, I don't know what we would do without you."

"Well, as long as Sharleen gets to stick around, I will, too."

"I'm working on that," Betty promised.

What exactly does that mean? Is my temporary job going to become a permanent one? God, I hope so.

Just outside of the converted classroom, the volunteers had formed a long line that trailed down the hall. Though their faces were filled with expressions of determination and hope, exhaustion was evident in their eyes.

Willie was walking the length of the line handing a paper plate to each person. "Be sure to grab a bottle of water, and there are napkins and utensils on the counter in the school office," she said as she continued her task. "Find a place to eat wherever you can. Grab a chair or a spot on the floor. Please help yourself to food. We appreciate all of you!"

The line started to move and people shifted forward. Sharleen stepped into the converted classroom, ready to help. The table she'd helped Joyce set up earlier that morning was now covered with food. Maisy was serving everyone a hearty serving of spaghetti, spooning it out from a huge pot. Victor and Ivy were in charge of serving scoops of salad to each person. Raquel and Camilla were on garlic bread duty. The mothers were ruling over the selection of homemade desserts, explaining to every volunteer they saw who baked what and whose recipe was the superior one. It was comedic chaos at its finest.

As the line started to thin, Maisy handed Sharleen a plate she'd prepared. "Here," she said. "I made this for you. I knew if I didn't, you'd find some excuse to not eat."

"I want to make sure everyone else gets to eat first," Sharleen protested, despite the fact the food looked and smelled amazing.

"I'm your boss," Maisy said. "Do what you're told. Eat."

Reluctantly, Sharleen took the plate, grabbed a bottle of water, and found an empty spot in the hallway to claim for herself. She sat and ate in silence. It wasn't long before distant memories stirred.

Sharleen's thoughts went back to a terrible afternoon. Right after the last recess of the day, young Holly and her circle of just-as-evil disciples cornered Sharleen, taunting her in a far corner of the old library. She remembered with vivid clarity the second Holly reached out and tugged at her hair, pulling hard.

"You're so dumb," Holly said, while the other girls behind her shrieked with laughter. "Who do you think you are, Beethoven?"

Sharleen looked down at her spaghetti lunch, grateful she was back in the hallway, grateful that the awful bullying she'd endured was behind her. For a moment she thought about Victor, making a mental note to find him before the day was through to see how he was doing.

Lunch. That was another memory. Sharleen turned and looked in the direction of the main entrance, recalling a time when her mother had rushed into the building with Sharleen's forgotten lunch in her hand. Young Sharleen had met her mother in the school office to receive the left-behind item. Theresa had bent down and kissed her daughter on the cheek. Sharleen inhaled deeply as she always did when her mother was near, smelling the sweetness emanating from her skin, a constant reminder of the local bakery Theresa worked at five days a week, sometimes having to be there as early as 5:00 a.m.

Still, she took the time to bring me lunch. That was just the kind of person she was. And exactly the same kind of person I want to be.

Sharleen closed her eyes to say a moment of thanks before taking her first bite, which tasted even better than it looked.

After lunch and spending a few minutes personally thanking every volunteer she could find, Sharleen walked outside and sat on the brick border of a flower bed. She stared at the wilted marigolds, wondering how they managed to stay alive in the winter air. The color of them seemed dull and lackluster, like they needed a pep talk in order to be revived.

Sharleen knew she was tense. She could feel it in her body, especially her muscles. While she craved a hot shower and a good night's sleep, she vowed to be the last one to leave the school for the night, in a show of solidarity with everyone who was working so hard.

Sitting alone, she zipped up her jacket and tried to conjure calming thoughts. Instead, moments from the last few weeks started to waltz through her mind, keeping her anxiety active and alive. Being able to relax had always been a struggle, but on this particular afternoon she really tried giving it her biggest effort.

After taking a few deep breaths, she closed her eyes and concentrated on the chilly air touching her skin.

Christmas is coming. My favorite holiday. My first one without my Lita. I hope I can make it through the day without falling apart. I miss her so much.

Sensing someone was nearby, Sharleen cracked open an eye and postponed any hope of relaxation.

A young man who looked to be in his late twenties was standing in front of her with a case of water bottles in his arm. He had an athletic build and exuded a sense of toughness.

"Taking a break?" he asked, as if they were close friends or co-workers.

"Only for a moment," Sharleen explained. "There's a lot of work to do inside." She gave him a look as if to say, Who are you?

Without being asked, he sat beside her, placing the case of water he carried on the ground at his feet. His closeness put Sharleen on guard. "I'm Michael Salazar," he said. "I'm Victor's dad."

Of course you are.

Sharleen breathed a quick sigh of relief. "Wow," she said. "It's nice to finally meet you."

He was a handsome man with a street-smart swagger. She wondered how much heartache he'd seen in his life. She sensed sorrow was lingering just beneath his macho surface.

"This might sound strange, but I feel like we already know each other," said Michael. "My wife and my son talk about you all the time."

Sharleen grinned. "That must drive you crazy."

"Yeah," he said with a nod. "Sometimes."

"Did you come here to help? Or for another reason?"

He took a breath and licked his lips. Sharleen wondered if this was a nervous habit of his. "I was sitting at home all alone and I realized how strange it must seem that I'm not here," he explained.

Sharleen decided to skip the small talk and get right to the point. She was tired and it showed in her words. "Do you want to be here?"

He turned and looked at her. She stared at his perfectly groomed dark goatee as he spoke. "I want to do the right thing, but it's hard for me," he said. "My son … he's different to what I expected. He and I don't have a lot in common."

"I think you do," she said. Michael looked confused. "It took a lot of courage for you to come here today, Mr. Salazar."

"Thank you. I appreciate you saying that. And you can call me Michael. Especially since my wife considers you family now."

"That's nice of you to say, but you three have been a family for a lot longer than I've been working at this school," she reminded him. "It sounds like you and Sylvia should have a talk about how much you both love your son. I suspect you both want to do right by him."

"Yeah, we do," Michael said. "I'm just not sure how. I mean, I know I haven't been the best dad to Victor … and I know I could do better."

"Have you talked to him?" she asked. Michael shook his head and lowered his eyes as if he were ashamed by his admission. "Well, I have," she continued. "And he's bright and kind and creative and I can tell he has a big heart. But, most importantly, I know Victor is forgiving. If you ask for it, he might give you that grace."

"Wow. I hear you're a really good teacher and now I can see why," he said, then added, "And I want to be a really good dad. I didn't have one of my own, so I screw up a lot. It's really not Victor's fault."

"Michael, we wouldn't be human if we didn't mess things up once in a while. I don't know a lot about being a parent. I don't have a child of my own. But I do know what it means to be someone's friend. Maybe that's what Victor needs right now … someone in his corner … someone he can trust. You seem like a very brave man."

"Yeah, I try to be."

"But it also takes a lot of courage for your son to dance. It's something he loves to do very much. And he's good at it. And with your support, he can only get better."

Michael slipped his hands into the pockets of his baggy coat. "I didn't realize how serious he was about it," he explained. "I've said some pretty awful things to him. I can't take those back."

Sharleen stood up. "No, you can't. But there is a lot of power in an apology, especially if it comes from the heart."

"That's really good advice," he said. "Thanks."

"Did you bring that water to donate?"

"I did."

"Come on," she said, as Michael got to his feet. "I'll show you where you can drop that off, and then … I'd like to show you something."

"Sounds good."

Sharleen led him into the building and to the first tall stack of cases of water bottles she saw.

"You can add that to this stack," she instructed. "We can never have enough water."

Michael added his case to the stack and noted, "I know you have a lot, but I should've brought more."

"Well, if you're interested in helping, we can always use another pair of hands," she said.

"Yeah, I'm happy to do whatever's needed."

"Are you good with a power tool?" she asked.

"I'm no professional," he said, "but I learn fast."

"I'll take you to meet the crew in a second, but first let's step in here."

Sharleen and Michael walked through a set of interior doors that opened up to a more secluded section of the main hallway, narrower and less polished than the section closer to the school office.

There, Victor, Raquel, Ivy, and Camilla were practicing the opening number together, under the watchful eye of Sylvia, who was playing the music for them through her cell phone and cheering them on. She was sitting in an uncomfortable looking chair, watching her son dance. There was a tender expression on her face, a look of admiration and pure love.

It was impossible to take your eyes off Victor, even in the low-lit makeshift rehearsal space that felt gray and gloomy. He was the bright spot. His energy and charisma emitted an aura that was seen and felt. It made you want to get up and dance because his passion for it was that strong.

Sharleen watched as Michael's gaze went to his son. In his eyes, she saw a beautiful moment of realization.

"He looks so happy," Michael said.

As soon as Victor saw and heard his father, he stopped dancing. He looked fearful, as if he'd been caught committing a crime.

Sylvia stopped the music. She seemed to snap into a state of preparedness and protection, like anticipating a battle she was ready for.

Instantly, the positive vibe the students had created with their joy of performing disappeared as if jealous ghosts had run down the hallway and stolen it from them before slipping through the barred windows and running loose on the playground.

"Dad?" Victor said. He'd only spoken one word, but the fact that he was afraid came through his broken tone, loud and clear.

Sylvia was on her feet. She stood between father and son like a human shield.

"Michael, what are you doing here?" she asked.

Michael stepped forward. He directed his words over Sylvia's shoulders, wanting them to reach Victor.

"It's okay, son," he said. "Don't stop dancing. Keep going."

There were tears in Victor's eyes then. Ivy reached out to him and placed a hand on his shoulder as though feeling the enormity of the moment and knew how badly Victor needed a friend. The sight of this made Sharleen start to cry, despite her effort to hold her tears at bay.

"Are you sure?" Victor asked, still scared.

"Yes," Michael said. "I'm positive."

Sylvia turned to her son. "That's right, Victor. You keep practicing," she said. She went to him and gave him a quick hug. "You're going to make us very proud when you perform in the show."

Everyone's eyes went to Michael when he said, "He already has."

Thank you, God. Thank you for this moment. Thank you for letting me bear witness to this.

Sylvia moved to where Sharleen and Michael stood. "You see, Sharleen. I told you my husband would come around eventually." Sylvia turned to her husband then and asked, "What took you so long?"

A second later, Sylvia pressed a button on her cell phone and upbeat holiday music filled the space around them, rolling and echoing down the long hallway. And Victor started to move. There was a new form of joy shining bright in his beautiful dark brown eyes.

TWENTY-TWO

I Saw the Light On

𝒜 WEEK PASSED AND each day felt like a blur. All of them leading to a shared victory.

The impossible just became possible.

The hour was late. Sharleen was alone in the multipurpose room standing in the center of the space. And already the tears were flowing.

While the layout was the same, the room itself had changed. New flooring. New stage. New tables and chairs. Even new curtains that were airy enough to let rays of light in, sun or moon.

Even the energy feels different, new.

Sharleen turned in a slow circle, taking it all in. She felt like a lost explorer who had stumbled upon a new world, the first to discover a beautiful place where magic was not only possible, it was inevitable.

Knowing Jake was due to pick her up out front any second, she checked the brand-new clock on the wall to see how much time she had.

Enough for one song.

Sharleen moved across the room and stopped at the new piano.

She paused a moment and whispered words of gratitude before she sat down.

She knew exactly what song to play, the one she'd written in honor of her parents. The same one Professor Richter had just given her an A on, as part of her final exam.

The first chord pierced her heart. The sound reverberated throughout the empty room, slicing the air with a note of hope.

Sharleen continued to play, letting the emotion flow through her, connecting with the keys. She produced a beautiful sound that filled every corner of the space around her.

The sound of the double doors clicking open caught her attention. She looked in that direction. Holly was standing there, bundled up in a coat and scarf, with a pair of bright red mittens sticking out of her pocket.

Immediately, Sharleen stopped playing. Silence once again filled the room.

Both women were quiet for a moment, their presence saying enough.

Finally, Holly spoke. "I don't recognize that tune," she said. "It's beautiful."

"It's something I wrote," Sharleen explained.

Holly took a few steps in Sharleen's direction. The sound of her shoes touching the shiny wooden floor echoed, like a warning.

Like an apology.

"I'm not really sure why I'm here," Holly began. Her voice was shaky. She sounded unsure, maybe even uncomfortable. "I was heading out for the day and I saw the light on. So ... I came inside ... because ... I knew I needed to. I knew you were in here."

"The room brings back a lot of memories," Sharleen said. "For both of us."

Holly took more steps, moving to Sharleen with a sense of hesitation and caution. "I need to say something to you."

Sharleen tensed. "I'm listening."

"I shouldn't have mocked you," Holly said. "The piano recital. I never should've done that to you."

"I remember that day well, Holly. This room was packed. I was up there on stage, ready to perform. My parents were here. My grandparents were here. My friends," Sharleen said. "And there was you. I could hear you in the crowd. Laughing and making other people laugh. At my expense. You were always good at that. Just because I loved to play the piano. Calling me ridiculous names. Pulling my hair. Punching me in the back. What did I ever do to you?"

"Nothing," Holly admitted. "You did nothing to me."

"Then why did you do it? And why do you still do it?"

"I was jealous of you," Holly said. "And clearly, I still am. I'm jealous of many people."

"You were a mean girl then and you're a mean girl now. Only one of us changed since grade school."

"I deserve that," Holly said. "I'm not perfect, Sharleen. I'm not proud of the way I've treated you or how I've acted."

"And to think, you're a teacher. You don't even deserve the honor of that title."

"Maybe not, but I'm here now. I'm standing in front of you because I need to face the truth ... about what I did ... what I put you through."

Sharleen stood. "I was only nine years old," she said. "How could you be so cruel?"

"That was your moment, and I ruined it," Holly agreed.

"Yes, you did. But you didn't ruin me."

"I tried," Holly said. "I did everything I could to break you."

"And you almost did."

"But you didn't break," Holly said. "Let's face it. You're a lot stronger than me. You were back then, and you certainly are now."

"I just don't understand why … playing the piano was the only thing I was good at back then. Why try and take that away from me?"

"But I didn't even have that," said Holly. "Sharleen, the only musical instrument I know how to play is the car radio." Holly took a breath. "Bad joke, I know … bad timing … but it's true. Do you know what I'd do to have a talent like yours?"

"Why did you help?" Sharleen asked. "Why did you make the effort? I honestly didn't think you cared about this school or anything else except for yourself."

"Well, I do care, believe it or not. And the fire was a horrible thing. And I thought what the community did was wonderful," Holly explained. "If you want to know the truth, all of this was a huge wake-up call for me, something I've needed for a long time."

"I need to go soon. Jake is waiting for me. And Ivy. We have plans tonight," Sharleen said. She grabbed her backpack and slid her arms through the shoulder straps. "Good night, Holly."

Sharleen headed for the door, but Holly's words stopped her. "I just want you to know … if I could take it all back … I would."

Sharleen turned back. In her mind, she saw a flash of Holly when she was younger, the ringleader of badness. The source of so much pain. "Holly, if you're here to apologize, there's no need," Sharleen said. "I forgave you a long time ago."

Holly locked eyes with her. The look they exchanged spoke volumes in silence, saying more than could ever be articulated. "Well, then you're one step ahead of me," said Holly. "I haven't forgiven myself." A tear slid down Holly's cheek. "I don't know if I ever will."

TWENTY-THREE

Showtime

THE NIGHT OF the show arrived quicker than Sharleen expected. All of a sudden it was here, and it was real. A part of her wished they had more time. Sure, the kids were more than ready to perform. They'd rehearsed around the clock. And Sharleen knew in her heart the show could mean great changes for the school. The collective effort to make it happen had been considerable and wouldn't have materialized without the rallying of the entire community. That journey still touched her. She was especially indebted to Jake and Maisy. Because of them, the multipurpose room was once again open and safe to use.

It hasn't even happened yet and I miss it already. The preparations. The hard work. The excited looks of anticipation on the beautiful faces of the students. I will miss all of this.

With only two hours to go before the curtain rose, Sharleen clicked open the double doors and stepped inside the brightly lit room. She was greeted by a flurry of activity.

The cafeteria tables and benches were folded upright, filed near the entrance to the now functional kitchen area. Willie and Joyce were placing folding chairs with careful precision. Sharleen did a double take, barely recognizing Willie, who had dressed up for the occasion in a charcoal gray power suit. Joyce teetered around in adorable high heels and a flowing lavender dress that looked both comfortable and elegant. There was a daisy in her hair.

Not far from the entrance to the room, Sylvia was putting the finishing touches on a vast arrangement of home-baked goods at a makeshift concession stand. There were more delicious treats to choose from than Sharleen could count. On display, an assortment of canned drinks and bottles of water occupied a corner. Sylvia was busy counting bills and change in a cash box. Her long hair was styled up for the occasion. Her beautiful pale teal dress embroidered with tiny rhinestone beads shimmered when she moved.

At a table near the window, Maisy was folding the printed programs for the show. She looked intent on getting the creases just right before placing them in a cardboard box with the others. She looked stylish and chic in a black cocktail dress, a very different look than her usual khakis and Polo. Spotting Sharleen enter the room, Maisy grinned and offered a welcoming wave.

"I've already taken my heels off," Maisy announced, "because my feet were killing me. Don't judge me."

"This is a judgment-free zone!" Sylvia shouted from across the room.

Behind Sharleen, Holly entered the room in a burst of energy, filling the space with her enthusiasm and frenetic pace. Dressed in black from head to toe and donning a headset to communicate with the backstage crew, she huffed across the room with a clip-board in one hand and a pencil in the other, looking very efficient, in full command. She was a little scary and possibly drunk with her new position of power.

"Let's move faster people!" she urged. "There's only two hours to showtime!"

Just as quickly as she had appeared, Holly climbed the steps and disappeared backstage.

The energy in the room shifted back to normal.

"Well, who put her in charge?" Joyce wondered aloud.

Willie stared in Sharleen's direction. "It wasn't my idea. Some-body made her the stage manager."

Sharleen smiled. "Somebody recognized Holly's impressive attention to detail and her ability to tell people what to do … dip-lomatically, of course."

"Diplomatically, my eye," Joyce said. "More like a holy reign of terror. Just so you know, we're all calling her Miss Bossy Pants."

"Among other things," Willie added with a mischievous smirk.

"Even though she's been a pain in the neck, I'm actually glad you gave Holly a chance," Joyce noted.

Sharleen smiled. "Me, too. She's actually been very helpful."

"Who knew?" Joyce tried to keep a straight face, but failed, giggling.

"Are you nervous?" Maisy asked Sharleen.

"Terrified, actually." Sharleen absentmindedly fidgeted with her hands until realizing, then stopped.

"Well, don't be," said Maisy. "The evening will be a big success. I can feel it in my tired Scottish bones. The little ones are so excited about the show. It's adorable. It kind of puts it all into focus, doesn't it … why we do the jobs we do. They make it all worth it."

Sylvia joined Sharleen in the center of the room, giving her a quick but needed hug. "Girl, that dress on you is everything," Sylvia raved. Sharleen spun in a circle to show the dress off in its entirety. "Red is definitely your color."

"I hope so. You don't think it's too much?"

"You look like the queen and you should," Sylvia said. "This night belongs to you."

"Thank you, but it's all for the kids," Sharleen said. "I want this to be a beautiful experience they'll never forget."

"And it will be," Willie said, joining them. "All because of you, Sharleen."

"Yeah," Joyce said from afar. "Even if you did put Miss Bossy Pants in charge. We all appreciate what you've done."

"We did this together," she reminded them.

"Group hug!" Sylvia suggested. Joyce happily moved in for the embrace, but Willie and Maisy looked hesitant. Sylvia speared them with a sharp look. "Okay, let me put it this way … if you don't get over here and let me hug you, I'm going to find you in the parking lot later tonight. And you know I will."

"Group hug!" Maisy said then, rushing to join.

"I'm only agreeing to this because I've seen Sylvia in action before and I know what's she capable of," Willie said. "That's why I'm glad I'm on her side."

"Girl, I'm your ride or die," Sylvia said. "We all are."

As they wrapped their arms around each other, their sweet laughter rose above to the ceiling and then rained back down on them, floating on invisible clouds of joy.

Moments later, Sharleen decided to check in with everyone backstage. The first person she saw was George, who was maniacally flipping through costumes hanging on a large rack.

Holly appeared, forehead creased in concern. "Everything okay?" she asked.

"It will be once I find a missing Santa hat. I know it's around here somewhere." He turned to Sharleen and said, "Next year, we're planning ahead."

Holly chimed in with, "I agree. Let's start planning next year's holiday show in July. We can never be too prepared."

"That sounds like a great plan," Sharleen said. "I'm really glad you two are here."

July. That sounds so far away. I hope I'm still here then. Right now, my job for the season ends at midnight.

"Thank you for giving us a chance," Holly said.

"You earned it. You both do."

"You might not know this," said George, "but you actually inspired me, Sharleen."

She raised an eyebrow, curious. "I did? How?"

"Because of you, I've decided to go back to school and get another degree. This one will be in costume design."

"Wow," she said. "That's awesome. I'm really happy for you, George."

Walking across the stage, Sharleen admired how beautiful the back of the red velvet and gold curtain was. She stopped to take in the behind-the-scenes view. For a moment, she imagined Alma there with her, wearing her favorite sapphire blue dress with the jeweled lace collar. Her long hair was pinned up in ribboned braids. They were standing on the stage together, with the hand-painted holiday set pieces serving as their backdrop.

"My ring," Alma said in Sharleen's imagination. "What did you do?"

"I did what I had to," Sharleen explained to the vision of her grandmother.

"I know, *m'ija*, and I'm very proud of you."

"I'm sorry about the ring, *Lita*. I'll get it back. I promise."

Alma reached out a hand to Sharleen, but their fingers didn't touch, their hands couldn't reach. "The everlasting gift," Alma said, already fading away. "That's what the ring is … for you."

"Thank you," Sharleen said, but it was too late. Alma was gone.

Sharleen shook off the moment and continued to move across the stage. She needed to check on the students and make sure they had everything they needed.

In the women's dressing room, the scene was full throttle pandemonium.

Holly entered behind Sharleen and gasped at the state of chaos. Clothes, makeup kits, and hair styling products were strewn about the messy room. There was a cacophony of chatter, quickly rising to an ear-splitting crescendo.

Lola, who was dressed to kill in a broad-shouldered white blazer and silk slacks, was helping her daughter get ready for the show, brushing her hair but struggling to tame Raquel's wild curls. Lola had slicked back her own hair for the occasion, giving her a look that resembled a female James Bond.

"Mom, do you have to brush so hard?" Raquel asked. "It hurts my head."

"If you sass me one more time, you won't live to see Christmas," Lola told her.

Raquel recoiled, making a face when Lola wasn't looking.

Sitting next to Raquel, Camilla was staring into the mirror. Her red hair was styled high, and a lot of makeup stole her pretty face. This combined effort resulted in her resembling a clown.

Cristina stood nearby looking at her daughter, horrified.

"Mother, why do you keep staring at me?" Camilla asked, eyes narrowed, head tilted, looking at her sideways.

Cristina swallowed and said, "Because I'm trying to figure out whose child you are."

Cristina was wearing a sparkly tuxedo jacket, a collared button-up blouse, and a pleated skirt. Her blonde hair was pulled up into a ponytail and glitter sparkled on her cheeks. She looked like a living doll.

"Let's keep the mood festive, ladies," Holly urged. "And please clean up after yourselves. This place looks like a disaster. This isn't a sorority house."

"Yes, Miss Holly," they replied in perfect unison.

Sharleen spotted Ivy sitting in a far corner of the room, alone and away from the crowd.

"Mind if I sit?"

Ivy shrugged. Sharleen sat in the empty chair beside her. "You look beautiful, Ivy."

Their eyes met in the mirror. Ivy managed a small smile. "Thank you, Miss Sharleen," she said. "So do you. Your dress is very pretty."

"It's hard sometimes, isn't it?" Sharleen asked. "Being the only girl in the room who doesn't have a mom. It doesn't feel fair."

Ivy gave this some thought. She gave another shrug and replied, "Yeah … I guess. But it's okay … now that you're here."

"I'm very proud of you. And I know your dad is, too. In fact, he might be convinced into taking us out for ice cream after the show."

Ivy's mood brightened. Her usual expression of happiness reappeared.

"I can't wait," she said. "I like it when we're all together."

"Me, too," Sharleen said. "Do you need me to get you anything? Some water, maybe?"

Ivy gestured to a bottle of water nearby. "No, thank you." She took a deep breath and leaned in close to Sharleen, glancing around at the other girls in the room nearby. "I'm very nervous. I've never sang in front of an audience before. I mean, I did at the school board meeting, but this is different. I'm scared."

"You're going to be awesome." Sharleen smiled, patting Ivy's hand.

"But what if I'm not?" Her smile reverted into a worried pout. "I don't want to ruin the show. Everybody will hate me."

Sharleen put a comforting arm around her shoulders. "From one performer to another, you can't let fear get the best of you," she said. "I want you to remind yourself about how much you love singing. And you go out there tonight and share your gift with the audience. Use your voice to bring them happiness. I know you can do this, Ivy. I have faith in you."

Ivy lowered her eyes, already fearing the worst. "And if I mess up?"

"Then you keep going," Sharleen said. "And you don't stop until the song is over."

"If I get really scared when I'm on stage, can I look at you? It will make me feel better if I know you're there."

"Of course," she said. "I'll be the lady in the red dress playing the piano, hoping I don't accidentally play something in the wrong key."

"Thanks," Ivy said. "That actually makes me feel better."

Sharleen started to stand up, but Ivy's words stopped her. "I'm really glad you met my dad," she said. "And me."

"Knowing both of you has made me very happy," Sharleen said.

As Sharleen headed to the dressing room door, she whispered in Holly's ear. "Can you gather the cast on stage in five minutes for a quick pre-show pep talk? I think they need one."

"You got it," Holly said, giving her a thumbs up.

Sharleen waited on stage for the students to join her. Once they were all there, she gathered them together, had them form a circle, and asked them to hold hands. To her surprise, none of them resisted.

She looked at them all, their young faces filled with excitement and nerves. How adorable they all looked in their costumes.

They've come so far.

Sharleen was already fighting to hold back tears of pride. "I just want to take a moment to say thank you."

The students looked confused. They stared at her as if they wanted her to elaborate.

"Thank us for what?" Raquel asked.

"Yeah," Camilla chimed in. "We should be thanking you, Miss Sharleen."

"Girls, let your teacher talk," Sylvia insisted from where she stood in the wing with Lola, Cristina, and Willie.

Sharleen turned to Victor, who was wearing his costume for the opening number, a candy cane striped shirt and green pants. His dark hair had been trimmed. She directed her words to him. "Thank you for teaching me to be brave when I forgot that I had courage," she said.

Victor looked into her eyes and said, "You're the bravest lady I know."

Sharleen then turned to Raquel and Camilla. "Thank you for becoming better versions of yourself, and for reminding me of the importance of forgiveness."

Both girls smiled back at her in response.

Sharleen looked down at Ivy, who was next to her and holding her hand. "And thank you for reminding me it's okay to be sad sometimes, as long as we remember that on the other side of darkness, there is light."

"I love you, Miss Sharleen," Ivy said with tears in her eyes.

"I love you, too." She looked at the students again. "I love all of you."

Willie stepped out onto the stage, appearing from the wing. "Miss Sharleen, you'll have to forgive me if I don't get my words right, but I'm so thankful that you walked through those doors last month."

"Yeah," Lola said, joining Willie on stage. "And you didn't leave when things got bad. That means a lot."

Sylvia and Cristina were there now, too. "And you put up with us and all of our kids," Sylvia said.

"And you don't make fun of the way I drive," Cristina said.

Everyone looked at her with an expression of confusion.

"And for being the coolest music teacher this school has ever had!" Cristina added.

The group on stage applauded in a show of appreciation for Sharleen.

Sharleen quieted them down before continuing. "I want each of you to enjoy every second you're on stage tonight because you've earned it. All of you have worked so hard. This is your moment. And I'm proud of each and every one of you," she said. "And, most importantly, I want you to have fun."

The audience arrived, including Jessica Spencer, the superintendent of the school board. Dressed impeccably, she was a silver-haired woman who exuded authority at a single glance. Peeking from behind the curtain on stage, Sharleen spotted her in the growing crowd, knowing who she was.

I need to talk to her. This is my last chance to convince her to help the school. It's now or never.

Sharleen hurried down the side steps and moved in the direction of where the superintendent stood, not far from the concession stand.

Before she knew what was happening, Betty appeared and locked arms with Sharleen. "Ready to impress?" she asked, walking with her.

Not sure what Betty meant exactly, Sharleen nodded.

Then, they were standing toe-to-toe with Jessica Spencer.

"Sharleen Vega," Betty began. "I'd like for you to meet our superintendent, Jessica Spencer."

Sharleen smiled and shook the woman's hand. "Hello, Superintendent Spencer. Thank you for being here tonight."

"It's nice to finally put a name to a face," Jessica said. Her no-nonsense expression melted into a warm smile. "I've heard a lot about you. It sounds like I missed quite a compelling speech at the last school board meeting. You made quite an impression, Miss Vega."

"About that," Sharleen said. "I just want to say—"

Jessica held up a hand. Sharleen couldn't help but notice the large rock on the woman's wedding finger and how perfectly polished her fingernails were. She was the epitome of class. "Say no more," insisted Jessica. "I firmly believe we have to stand up and fight for the things that matter to us."

"Yes, I agree," said Sharleen. "And that's why I'm very grateful to you for being here. There's so much I want to say to you, but I don't want to take up a lot of your time."

"It's no secret this school needs some additional support," Jessica conceded. "You'll be pleased to know Principal Marchant and I have a meeting scheduled early next week to discuss the matter in great detail."

"I'm happy to hear that," Sharleen said. "I just hope our students can inspire you by their performance tonight to consider helping them secure as many fair opportunities as possible. They only want the same chance to succeed that other students have at other schools. They shouldn't be punished because of their zip code."

"Very well said," Jessica said. "I like your passion, Miss Vega."

"We wouldn't be standing here tonight without it," Betty added.

"By the way, Robert Kellis is here tonight with me," Jessica explained. She gestured to the audience where Robert sat. He glanced in their direction and stood when he saw them. He was dressed in a beautiful suit and a festive tie. He waved at Sharleen and smiled at her from the distance. She returned the friendly gesture with a smile and a wave of her own.

"That's very nice of him to be here," Sharleen said to Jessica. "It means a lot that you both showed up ... more than you can know."

"Robert said to me he wouldn't miss this show for anything," Jessica offered. "And I have to say, I agreed with him. Thank you for all your hard work, Miss Vega. You truly have made a difference."

The lights in the multipurpose room suddenly flickered. Betty glanced up, concerned.

"Oh no," she said. "I hope it's not another issue with the wiring. The last thing we need is another fire."

"No need to worry," Sharleen assured her. "The lights ... it means it's almost showtime. If you'll excuse me, I have a piano to play and the two of you have a performance to watch. Superintendent Spencer, it was a pleasure to meet you."

"Likewise. I'm sure we'll see each other again soon."

Sharleen moved across the room and took her seat at the piano. Once there, she exhaled a big sigh. The conversation with the superintendent had gone better than expected. Sharleen felt hopeful the lady would keep her word and find the needed resources.

She reached into her backpack, which was on the floor near her feet, fished out a bottle of water and took a sip. She then cracked her knuckles, took a few deep breaths, and spent a moment taking a quick look at her sheet music.

She heard Professor Richter's voice before she saw her.

"Straighten your posture, Sharleen," commanded Lena. "You're a piano player, not a saloon girl."

Sharleen stood up to greet her teacher. "Professor Richter, you're here!"

"Of course I am," she said. "You've done a good thing. A real good thing."

"I hope so," Sharleen said. "To tell you the truth, I'm shaking like a leaf on the inside, but trying my best to keep it together."

"Remember what I've taught you … take the nervousness and turn it into excitement. It's a gift to be able to do what we do."

"A gift," Sharleen repeated. "That's exactly what this night feels like. I feel blessed."

The professor's usual stoic expression softened. "Beverly Schwartz might've won the scholarship," she said, "but it looks to me like you've won a lot more. Even without a tambourine."

"You couldn't be more right," Sharleen agreed, a triumphant smile replacing nervous jitters for the time being.

"It's quite a turnout for this event," Lena said, glancing around the room. "Look at all the people you've been able to bring together. It's no secret you're going to be an exceptional teacher one day, Sharleen."

"Thank you. For everything. You've been a great teacher to me and a wonderful friend."

"There's no need to thank me," Lena insisted. "You did all the work."

"Speaking of," Sharleen continued. "About the job in the piano lab…"

Lena gave her a look. "I think it's safe to say you've outgrown that position. For what it's worth, I'm proud of you. I'm sure your parents and your grandmother would be, too."

I hope so. I know they're watching over me right now. And always.

Professor Richter left to find an empty seat in the audience.

Jake arrived then, with a bouquet in each hand. He kissed Sharleen's cheek.

"I don't even recognize you," she said. "A suit and a tie and dress shoes? Who are you?"

"I told you I clean up well," he said with a grin. "And you … that dress … you're stunning, Sharleen. The most beautiful woman in the room … and you're mine. I'm a very lucky guy."

"Ah, I bet you say that to all the girls," she joked. Her attention moved to the flowers he held. "Are one of those for me?"

"Yes, but you can't have them until after the show."

"Fair enough. By the way, how did you know carnations are my favorite?" she asked.

"Lucky guess."

"I'm the lucky one, Jake."

"We both are," he said. "We found each other in the middle of this crazy world."

"We did," she agreed. "And now I'm never letting you out of my sight."

He bent down and gave her another kiss. "Break a leg … isn't that what they say?"

"You smell good," she said. "Like expensive cologne … and sin … my future."

"Both can be arranged." He offered a sly grin.

"Want to take Ivy out for ice cream after the show?"

He laughed. "I think she'll insist on it."

"Then it's a date," she said. "Besides, I already told her it was happening and that it was your idea."

The lights in the audience dimmed.

"I love you, Sharleen," he said.

She stared into his dark eyes. "I love you, too."

Jake turned away and hurried back to his seat.

On stage, the curtain came up. As rehearsed, the students were on stage and in position for the opening number.

Sharleen whispered a silent prayer, played the first few chords of the classic song, and the show began.

She watched with immense glee as the students sailed through the choreography and hit each sung note with perfection. Victor's elegance and grace shone through as he moved around the stage, dancing better than ever. The crowd was mesmerized by him, watching him with awe.

Up next, the mothers took the stage. Sylvia was in the center of their inverted triangle, taking the lead on a famous holiday song, while Lola and Cristina were her backup. They were the perfect trio. Their voices blended together in perfect harmony, bringing the crowd to their feet in a show-stopping moment. Tears streamed down their faces as their performance came to an end, basking in the deserved adoration of their cheering audience.

Next was a skit that explored the many meanings of the holiday season. In it, Willie made a cameo appearance dressed as Santa Claus. George was her faithful and hilarious sidekick, dressed like an overgrown elf. Together, their wild antics on stage resulted in rounds of laughter.

The students were back on stage next to perform a medley of holiday songs while decorating a Christmas tree. The number was sweet and sentimental.

Sharleen glanced out at the audience and noticed that Jessica looked pleased with the show.

This is a good sign. She's going to help the school. I can feel it.

Ivy entered the stage with a microphone in hand. Raquel and Camilla followed her on stage as her backup singers. Before the music began, Ivy looked at Sharleen, who smiled and gave her an encouraging thumbs up. Ivy waved at her in response. She took a deep breath and then sang the opening verse of the song. By the time she reached the chorus, her confidence was in full bloom. She moved back and forth across the stage with ease. During a musical break, Victor took center stage and wowed the crowd with a hip-hop dance solo.

The show flew by. The next thing Sharleen knew, the students were on stage performing the high energy and very inspiring closing number. They hit their final poses. The lights went out. The show came to an end.

The outpouring of love for the students in the form of applause was almost deafening, touching every wall in the renovated room and shaking any remaining gloom out of the school forever.

On stage, the stage lights came back up. The students lined up shoulder to shoulder, prepared to take a bow. They were surprised by the thunderous applause from the audience, followed by a standing ovation, which was initiated by Victor's father, who was the first one on his feet. A few students began to cry tears of happiness, overwhelmed by the immense emotions they were feeling and the intensity of the moment.

The crowd settled down when Ivy stepped forward and spoke into her microphone. "Thank you very much for being here tonight and for being such a great audience," she said. Sharleen started to panic, knowing none of what was happening had been rehearsed. "None of us would be here today without our favorite teacher.

Well, she's not really a teacher yet, but to us, she already is." Ivy looked for Sharleen, shielding her eyes from the bright lights with the edge of her hand. Then, she found Sharleen, looked at her, and said, "We love you, Miss Sharleen."

Encouraged by the audience's outburst of more applause, Sharleen stood up from the piano, climbed the steps, walked to center stage, and took a bow.

To Sharleen's surprise, Ivy handed her the microphone.

Sharleen wiped her eyes before she spoke, praying she would get her words right. "I can't thank everyone enough who believed in this show and the talent of these students," her voice trembled with emotion. "You came together and you made this happen. Not even a fire could stop us. I must tell you that the biggest lesson a soon-to-be-teacher can ever learn is the one taught by her students. To believe that the impossible is possible. And I really do. With all my heart. I hope all of you have very happy holidays."

Sharleen was prepared to exit into the wing, but Jake suddenly appeared on stage. He joined Sharleen, standing next to her.

"Sharleen Vega…" he said.

What is he doing?

Jake dropped down to one knee. Realizing what was about to occur, the audience responded, leaning forward in their chairs like a wave. Several gasps were heard.

Sharleen couldn't hold back her tears any longer.

"You've already made me the happiest man alive," he said. "You've taught me to let go and to love again. Before I met you, I thought I would never know joy again. I'm asking you to become my wife so we can spend the rest of our lives together." Jake took a deep breath before he said, "Sharleen Vega, will you marry me?"

From his pocket, Jake took out a small white velvet box. He opened it to reveal Alma's ring.

At the sight of the ring, Sharleen looked up briefly, knowing that Alma was somehow responsible for everything that was happening at that moment.

Thank you, Lita.

Sharleen reached out and touched Jake's cheek. "You went and got it back?" she asked through her tears.

"Yes," he said. "Because I'd do anything for you."

For a brief moment, they spoke in silence, looking deep into each other's eyes.

"Yes, Jake Arlington," Sharleen said. "I will marry you."

"Yes?" He jumped up to his feet.

"Yes!" she shouted.

The audience erupted into applause, cheering them on.

Sharleen and Jake embraced. They stopped and reached for Ivy and pulled her into their hug. Ivy clung to them, crying.

Backstage, the mothers were holding hands and weeping with joy.

"Hey, do you think she'll ask us to be her maids of honor?" Lola asked, sniffling.

"If she knows what's good for her, she will," said Sylvia.

TWENTY-FOUR
Merry Christmas

SHARLEEN STOOD NEAR the double doors, thanking people and saying goodbye to them as they left.

Maisy was one of the last people to leave. "You did an outstanding job, Sharleen."

"Despite the challenges?"

"Challenges mean nothing to you. I had a hunch about you and I was right," Maisy said. "But, then again, I usually am."

Maisy moved to leave but Sharleen reached out and touched the sleeve of her cocktail dress, stopping her. "Thank you for the opportunity, Maisy. You believed in me when no one else did and I'll be grateful to you for that … for this … for the rest of my life." Sharleen looked around the room, taking it all in. "I only wish this job was a permanent one."

Maisy grinned, patted her on the back, and said, "I have a feeling that wish is about to come true. And, when it does … be sure you're on time."

With that, Maisy left.

Betty approached Sharleen. She was smiling from ear to ear. "Bravo," she said. "A job well done. A week ago, I didn't think any of this was possible, but you proved me wrong. You're the best backup principal I could ever ask for."

"Thank you," Sharleen said. "I didn't get a chance to say goodbye to the superintendent and Mr. Kellis. Did they like the show?"

Betty's eyes brightened. "They loved it."

"Do you think they'll help us?" Sharleen asked, eager to hear the right response.

"We're breaking ground on a new library and a new performing arts center in March," Betty explained.

"Oh, Betty, that's wonderful. This is the best news ever."

"It is," Betty agreed. "There was only one condition to the terms."

"I'm afraid to ask," Sharleen said.

"Jessica Spencer said you had to be there to make sure it happens."

She stared at Betty in disbelief. "What do you mean? Are you offering me a job?"

Betty nodded. "I am. I would be a fool not to."

Inside, Sharleen felt her hope dim. "But I still have another semester of college," she reminded Betty.

"Those are semantics. Until then, I'm sure we can figure something out." Betty reached into her purse. "Speaking of which, this is for you." She handed Sharleen an envelope.

"What is this?" she asked, turning it around, checking for an address, a name, something.

"It's your tuition," Betty explained. "You have Willie to thank for this. It was her idea. The entire neighborhood took up a collection. Apparently, they want you to get your degree, no matter what."

Sharleen smiled and held the envelope to her heart. "Yes," she said. "No matter what."

It was Christmas morning. The hour was early. The smell of cinnamon-flavored pancakes and fresh-brewed coffee was heavy in the air.

Jake, Sharleen, and Ivy gathered around the Christmas tree, cherishing the start of a new tradition.

As Ivy opened her gifts, Jake and Sharleen shared a silent exchange, a tender look of love.

Sharleen glanced down at the ring on her finger.

The everlasting gift.

Though her parents and Alma weren't there to share in the joy of the day, she felt their presence. She knew they were watching over her.

Now and always.

Sharleen's attention shifted to the Christmas tree. For a moment, she watched the lights, lost in thought and the repetitive rhythm of the beautiful blinking colors. She turned slightly and glanced at the photo booth pictures of her parents, nestled between two branches of the pine tree. Next to the picture was a new ornament, an adorable porcelain cow.

Sharleen smiled, looked at her beautiful new family, and said to them, "Merry Christmas."

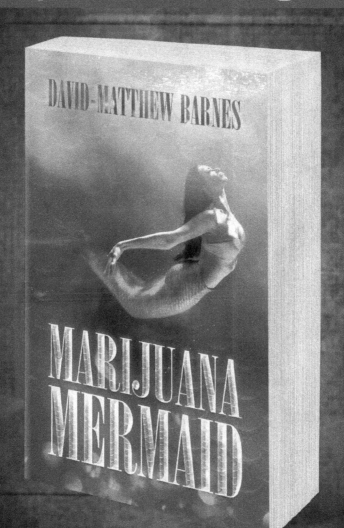

MORE READS

CayellePublishing.com

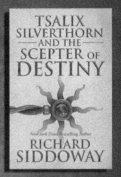

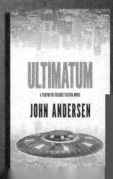

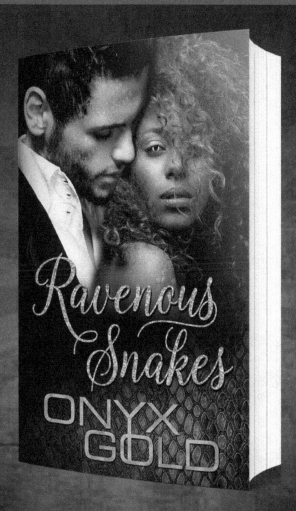